He Beats Me

A

Rod Cornelius

Story

Copyright © Rod Cornelius, 2017
An Akirim Press Publishing
Copyediting By Mirika Mayo Cornelius/Akirim Press

www.akirimpress.com
www.rodcornelius.com

He Beats Me

When Ashley first met Keon, she thought she had met the love of her life. It wasn't long after she cut herself off from all of her family and friends that Keon revealed his true abusive nature. Ashley quickly went from being the target of his affection to the target of his strikes and stomps. It's not until Keon's big move into the drug game goes tragically awry that he realizes the usefulness for Ashley again. The problem is, if he can't get his plan to work, they all could end up dead.

More Akirim Press Books

<u>Books by Rod Cornelius</u>

Diggin' Gold

The Trusted

Single Again

Ghetto Eyes

The Best Kept Secrets

When It Comes Around

UGLY

Whatever It Takes

<u>Books by Mirika Mayo Cornelius</u>

Secret

Colored Lily: Poppa Took My Innocence

Ain't Quite What I Thought

Ain't Quite What I Thought 2

Sunny Sides of My Shade

Murders At Gabriel's Trail: The Complete Series

First Degree Sins

Paton

<u>Books by Cyan Deane</u>

Dead Man's Mayhem

Execution's Karma

Table Of Contents

He Beats Me

When her eyes parted, she had no idea how long she had been lying there, dead to the world. A sharp jolt of pain ravaged throughout her body as she cautiously lifted her face from the cold, hard floor. She let out an agonizing moan as she rose to her feet and backed up onto the edge of the bed. With her head ringing and her entire body sore, it all suddenly came back to her–he beat her again.

After taking a few moments to gather herself while caressing the small lump on the side of her head, she carefully crept into the bathroom. She grabbed a towel, threw it in the sink and ran the water. She gazed at herself in the mirror as she contemplated her reason for allowing him to do this to her again. While examining her face for any noticeable bruises other than her small lump, she despised the reflection looking back at her that actually found relief in the fact that he didn't leave any visible marks on her face this time.

She picked up the towel, but before she could wipe her face with it, she burst into a fit of tears. She couldn't understand why he always found reasons to hurt her when all she ever wanted him to do was love her—nothing more, nothing less. All she wanted, all she ever asked from him, was his love.

Flashes of him with his hands around her neck as she helplessly struggled to breathe and claw herself out of his overwhelming grasp replayed through her mind. The demented smirk on his face as he forced her into unconsciousness was etched within her head. His words, "I should kill you right now, bitch," that slithered from his lips while they were pressed snugly against her cheek, still rang in her ears.

The thought of him gaining pleasure from tormenting her was enough to have her march from the bathroom and rush to her closet. She ripped her clothes from the racks and threw them onto the bed.

She then turned to her dresser, grabbed as much of her items as she could from the drawers and tossed them onto the bed also. Dropping to the floor, she dragged out her only suitcase from underneath the bed and slapped it onto the mattress. She flung it open and threw everything she could into it as quickly as possible. As she filled the suitcase, reality swiftly struck, and it slowed her down. *Was there any way to completely disappear from him? Where in the hell would I go? Who would help me?* She managed to cut herself off from the rest of the world over the past few years, wagging around with this man that somehow found it so easy to put her through so much pain.

She froze. The anger that spread throughout her body was nearly impossible for her to contain as she propelled her suitcase onto the floor. She dropped onto the bed and buried her face into her pillows. It was the pillows that muted the screams that bellowed from deep in her gut as she laid there punching into the mattress while crying to herself. She felt so helpless, so weak, and so alone.

Her sadness and anger was quickly transformed into fear when she heard the door slam from the front of the apartment. She briskly hopped up from the bed, scurried into the bathroom and twisted the faucet off to stop the water she had left running. She then made her way to the bed in an attempt to clean up the mess she had made with her clothing, but the bedroom door sprang open. She halted as he eased into the room through the door carrying a single red rose.

"Hey, Ma," he greeted her.

"Keon," she answered nervously.

"Baby, I'm sorry," he said as he approached her. "I know I said I wasn't gonna get mad like that no more, and I winded up doing it again. Man, I know I fucked up."

"It's…" she stopped as her heart pounded ferociously while he approached. For once, he actually sounded sincere, but she knew if he assessed that she was trying to leave him, his mood would swing in the blink of an eye and all hell would break loose. He always made it his business to tell her that it wasn't going to be a good thing if she ever left him. He warned her that the people she loved the most would get hurt, and she would most definitely feel his unforgiving and complete wrath–if she was lucky. With his aggressive behavior, she didn't have any reason not to believe him. She couldn't keep her eyes from wandering towards the mess all over the floor behind him as another empty apology bounced from his lips.

"Nah, nah, it's not okay. Take this," he said as he handed her the rose and swallowed her with a hug. "I ain't shit to be taking my anger out on you like that–as good as you are to me."

"Keon, don't worry about it," she said.

"Nah, baby," he said as he backed away from her. "This shit I got going on got me so fucked up right now. I need to treat the people who really got my back with the most care. I can't be doing this shit to you."

"Keon, really," she said. "I understand."

"Nah, baby, I ain't shit," he said as he threw up his hands and turned away from her. When his eyes fell on all the clothing that was scattered across the bed, they quickly zoomed across the room to the suitcase and all of Ashley's remaining garments hanging out of it. "You 'bout to fucking leave me?"

It was almost like she got punched in the gut; the air left out of her body so quickly. She didn't know how to answer him as she just fumbled on a few sounds of gibberish. She knew the sight was enough to set him off again. "Keon, I…" Before she could get another word out, the back of his hand cracked the side of her face.

"Really bitch? You fucking trying to leave me?" he asked. His face was filled with rage. His high yellow complexion turned beet red as he scowled at her with his fists balled.

"Keon… don't," she cried with one hand against the side of her face and the other held up high in an attempt to block the barrage of punches she was expecting to follow.

He slowly raised his hand as if he was about the smack the daylights out of her, but he opted to just shove her away from him instead. He said, "I done told you before. You ever leave me, not only am I gonna take your ass out, but I'm gonna take out some of your people, too. You think I'm playing with you about that shit? You think I'm a liar?"

"No, Keon," she said. "I believe you."

"Then why the fu…" he said, directing his finger towards the side of her head, then smashing it into her temple as hard as he could. "Just give me back my shit." He snatched the rose from her, balled it up and threw it right back at her.

"I'm sorry, Keon."

"You right about that. Your ass is sorry as hell," he said. "Just go'on and take your lousy ass in there and cook me that steak I just brought in there. Make sure you cook that shit well, too. I'm a black

13

man. I ain't no goddamn peckerwood. I don't like no damn bloody ass meat. Last time you cooked me a damn steak, the shit could've donated blood. You hear me?"

She nodded nervously, careful to not make eye contact with him again as she hustled towards the door. "Yes, I hear you, Keon."

"And cook both of 'em, too. I brought one for your disloyal ass, too, feeling all sorry for your ass. So since your ass up in here thinking about leaving a nigga, I'mma eat yours, too–right in front of your trifling ass. Them damn corn flakes is gonna be your meal tonight, and you better not touch another crumb of any other food but them damn corn flakes, too."

"That's fine, Keon," she said with her head still hanging downwards, somewhat grateful he didn't make things physical again.

"I know it's fine. Now make the shit snappy," he yelled. She quickly left the bedroom door as he just shook his head, disgusted by her existence.

****

As he chomped and smacked on the well done T-bone steaks she prepared for him, she quietly stared at the knife that resided beside his hand. She didn't want him to see her staring at it for too long or too often, but she couldn't keep her eyes off of it. She hadn't even touched the bowl of cereal that sat in front of her that he demanded she prepare for herself for supper. The desires to reach across that table, grab the knife and stab him right in his throat were just running too rampantly through her mind for her to have any kind of appetite.

Just one poke in the right place, that's all it would take for her to be free from the evil shadow he reigned so heavily over her life. But she was too scared. She thought with her luck, he'd beat her to the flippin' knife and stab her with it as fast as she could jump for it. Or even worse, she'd grab it and somehow fall on top of the sharp object, puncture herself and just bleed to death, knowing Keon would no doubt graciously watch the blood ooze straight from her body until her final breath.

No, if there was one thing she understood about herself, it was that she was no killer. No matter how bad Keon would beat or abuse her, she just didn't have it in her to end his life, even though the opportunities seemed plentiful. More importantly, she understood she just couldn't allow things to go on like they were with his violent treatment towards her because eventually he was going to wind up killing her. She knew it. There wasn't a day that went by that she didn't have fears about it. Every morning she woke up, she thought this was going to be the day she'd die by his ratchet hands. When her eyes trailed upwards, Keon's eyes were locked on hers.

"You getting some ideas?" he asked with a slow chew matched with a pair of suspicious eyes.

"No," she uttered nervously, somewhat afraid that he could somehow see her thoughts with his evil stare.

With a nod and a chuckle, he said, "If you feeling froggish, go'on head and jump. Now when your ass jump, you better jump like a motherfucker though, because when I catch you, and believe me when I tell you this shit–I will catch you, I'm gonna put your ass in so much pain and agony, you gonna wish you ain't never crossed my yellow ass. You're gonna beg me just to kill your dizzy, black ass. I promise you that."

She just shook her head while he gazed at her, smirking. She couldn't believe the words that managed to escape from the lips of the man with whom she once wanted to spend the rest of her life. As his wicked eyes rested on her, she prayed that God would just do her a divine favor of having a piece of that savory steak she had just prepared for him to slip and get stuck down the wrong pipe and choke him right dead, finally freeing her of the misery of being with him.

His last disrespectful statement made it just too difficult for her to resist asking him, "What happened to you?"

"Bitch, ain't shit happened to me. You need to be asking your damn self that question. Me–I just finally started realizing that you're a goddamn disappointment. When we first met, I really thought you were a ride or die chick, but eventually, I realized all the fuck you do is die. You're like a pack of fucking Dollar Store batteries. Put 'em in, and their ass will work great for about fifteen minutes, but then all the sudden they just die on a nigga–completely fucking useless–just like you in every way imaginable. Anymore fucking questions?"

His words forced her to fight back her tears. She couldn't look at him any longer. Although she fell out of love with him long ago, his words still cut deep. He hated her with all his soul and somehow she still had something in her heart for him.

There was a knock at the front door. He looked back at the door and then back at her. She knew that was her signal to go answer it. She hopped up out of her chair, but before she could make her way towards the door, he grabbed her arm. "Look here, you look through that fucking peephole before you open that goddamn door. Don't act like your nosey ass don't know what's going on."

"I will," she replied. She scurried to the door, and as he instructed, she looked through the peephole. When she opened the door, Porkchop was standing on the other side of it.

The tall, lanky man with a low box haircut proceeded to speak, "Hey, Ashley. Keon here?"

She stepped back from the door and threw her hand out in Keon's direction towards the dining area on the other side of the apartment. Before closing the door behind him, she stuck her head out of the door to see if anyone else was downstairs.

"Goddamn dude, where you been at?" Porkchop asked as he hurried towards the kitchen table.

"Minding my own fucking business, nigga," he said while slicing his meat into smaller chunks.

Porkchop took a seat at the table and said, "Damn, that smells good."

"It is good, nigga," he laughed. "The old lady can cook her ass off when she's motivated."

"You got some more of that?"

"The hell this look like, a restaurant or something?"

"Nah, man, I was just asking."

"Well nah, we ain't got no more," Keon spat. "Anyway, nigga, you heard anything from, Angelo?"

"Hell, you heard anything from him?"

"Hell no, that's why I'm asking you. I thought that's what I sent you to do anyway–to find his thieving ass."

"Man, I can't track that nigga nowhere. Nigga got three baby mommas and eight kids, and ain't none of 'em even seen or heard from him. It's like the nigga just vanished into thin air."

"Really?" Keon asked as he dropped his fork and just gazed at Porkchop.

Ashley grabbed the remote control off of the coffee table in the living room area behind them and flipped on the television, but before her bottom could hit the couch, Keon called, "Ashley, this trash shole looking full over here."

She took a deep breath and dropped the remote on the coffee table. "I'll get it."

She walked over to the trash can as Keon still had his eyes locked on Porkchop, not flinching an inch. The stare made Porkchop feel uneasy, so uneasy that he took his eyes off of Keon and glanced over to Ashley and the trash bin.

"And don't forget you got some shit to clean up back there in that bedroom when you get back," Keon added.

She didn't respond as she tied the ends of the big, black trash bag and struggled carrying it to the front door.

"Damn, blood, you got your old lady taking out the trash in the middle of the night? You raw as hell."

"What's it to you, nigga?"

"Nothing… I mean... nothing."

"Alright then," said Keon. "At least she can do what the hell I send her out to do, unlike some other motherfuckers."

"Man, the last thing we need to be doing is jumping down each other's throat."

"Nigga, I ain't jumping down nobody's throat, and you damn shole ain't jumping down mine."

"I'm just saying."

"Don't just say shit. Just explain to me how in the hell you come back with nothing on this nigga? Speak on that shit."

"Man, look, we've been looking for this dude for over two weeks now. We ain't gonna find him. We just need to haul ass like he did before Max sends his goons out lurking like we both know he's gonna do."

"Haul ass? Haul ass to where?"

"Why is you playing with dude?"

"Playing with dude? I ain't playing with nobody, bruh. This nigga breathe and bleed just like I do. My heart don't pump no Kool-aid. Yours might do, but not mine."

"Nigga, if mine did, I don't wanna be laid up nowhere leaking blood and guts to find out."

"What? So you think you can hide from niggas like Max? How long do you think it would be after you go calling yourself *hauling ass* before one of his dudes show up wherever you think you're hiding at, ready to split your damn wig?"

"Well it's better than being a sitting duck!"

"Nah, hell with that. I got a plan."

"A plan, huh?"

"That's what the hell I said," Keon replied with a slow nod and smirk on his face.

When Ashley stepped onto the sidewalk leading out from her building, she couldn't help but notice a black sedan backed into a parking space with no other cars around it. There appeared to be two figures inside the vehicle, and the occupants seemed to be looking right at her. She bowed her head, walked off the sidewalk and into the street slowly. Her gut was telling her they were staring at her building, possibly even looking for Keon about whatever crap he found himself into this time. Her nerves had her praying that they wouldn't try to shoot her to get back at him because that would most definitely be a fail. She figured if they did that, they'd only be doing him a favor, yet in a twisted way, doing her one, also.

With the big, black bag of garbage in her hand, she tried her best to keep the car in her periphery and not look directly at it. When she walked in front of the car, the car started and sprang its bright lights right on her. She froze. The car pulled slowly out of the parking space. Her heart raced as she accidently looked right into the face of the brawn white man with his big, scruffy red mustache in the driver seat. She couldn't take her eyes off of his cold, pale face as the black car simply passed her by.

"Please tell me that shit you just told me ain't really your plan."

"No, that's exactly what the plan is."

"Nigga!" Porkchop jumped up out of his chair and threw his hands in the air. "What in the world

25

makes you think Ashley's momma is gonna give you eighty grand when she don't even like your ass? None of her family does."

"She's not gonna give it to me. She's gonna give it to Ash."

"The woman you just made drag a big ass bag of trash out to the dumpsters all by herself in the middle of the night?"

"Negro, calm down with all that yelling in my house like that. Where the hell you think you're at?"

Porkchop took a deep breath and sat back down at the table with his partner in crime, staring wildly at him.

"Alright now, nigga, I told you I got a plan. I got it all worked out with Ashley. Hell, I know her people don't like me. I can't stand none of their snooty asses neither," he continued while digging into his food again, "But they love Ashley. We're gonna tell her momma we need the money to put a nice down payment on a house."

"A house with you?"

"You got any better ideas?"

"Yeah, getting the hell out of dodge."

"Porkchop, we ain't running nowhere. Now, didn't you say that nigga Angelo got three baby mommas and eight little ones?"

"Yeah."

"And don't that chick Keisha we know from way back got five rug rats with that nigga?"

"Yup."

Keon took a moment to think. "She locked the nigga up a few times for not paying child support, too."

"Yup, that's her."

"Alright then, I need you to go back and put some major pressure on her ass. Scare her ass up, do whatever the hell you have to do to make her give you a lead on this chump. Maybe even try and bribe one of them rug rats of hers with some gummy bears or some shit," he said. "A nigga with that many seeds in one spot is gonna keep his ass close to the nest with the highest potential child support payment. Besides, if we can find that nigga maybe we can beat his ass until he tell us what he really did with that money, and we can get that shit back."

"And when we don't find him and you don't get the money from Ashley's family, then what are we gonna do? Max is giving us till Friday to have his money, and nine out of ten that cat ain't really gonna give us that long. We're probably already on the chopping block as we speak."

"Nigga, stop being so damn pessimistic," said Keon. He turned towards the door when he heard Ashley returning through it and whispered to his partner. "If shit falls through, then I got a contingency plan. I got my cuz down in Rock Hill. He got some connects where he can get us a clean ride, some credit cards and a couple of fake IDs, but if shit goes like it should, we won't have to worry about none of that. You feel me?"

Porkchop, still weary of the plan, nodded in agreement. "Alright, I'll follow your lead."

"Good," he said. "Porkchop, I need your head in the game, bruh. I can't get through this shit if we're not on the same page. We're in this shit together, my nigga."

He nodded again and said, "Alright... I'm game."

****

Ashley sat on the bed drifting off at the television as Keon took his shower. Dinner at her mother's house the following day was stuck in her mind. She figured there was no possibility on God's green earth her mother was going to give them the amount of money Keon was putting her up to ask for. Besides, her mother and the rest of the family had always known Ashley to be the loner type and never the one to ask anyone for anything. It was one of the reasons her relationship with the family was so strained in the first place, in addition to leaving and shacking up with a man they all collectively considered to be no good.

Keon eased out of the bathroom with a towel around his waist and his frame still dripping wet. He immediately walked to the edge of the bed, picked up the remote and cut off the television.

"You know if you work this thing out for me, it will make me forget about the stunt you tried to pull on me earlier today. Matter of fact, I won't ever bring the shit up again. It'll be like the shit never happened."

"About the money, Keon, I don't think…"

He cut her off. "At-at-at, don't you call yourself up in here talking about you're thinking. That's what I do. I do all the thinking around here. Now, when your daddy passed away, out of all his kids, you ain't get shit, and you and I both know, it's well beyond time for you to collect what's due to you."

"But Keon, my momma's not gonna buy this story you want me to tell her."

"Well, you better sell the shit as best you can, because I'm tellin' ya', it ain't gonna be a good thing if we don't get this money, Ash. I'm just gonna be straight with you."

All Ashley could do was shake her head as he marched out of the bedroom and into the living room. Keon was bent on making something happen that just wasn't going to happen. It would be a cold day in hell before her mother would give her anything while she was still with the man she believed was abusing her own flesh in blood. It was the only reason she didn't receive any of her inheritance from her father when he passed years ago, and it would remain the reason she wouldn't receive any of it now.

****

Ashley checked herself out in the mirror one last time to make sure the bump on her head from the day before was no longer visible. It wasn't. Relieved, she charged through her bedroom, grabbed her purse from the bed and headed for the front door. When she placed her hand on the doorknob, she paused. She quickly remembered where she was headed and what she was about to be put up to do. Armed with an idea failed at its creation, Ashley hustled over to the phone and dialed her mother's house. The phone rang three times, and after a soft hello, Ashley slammed the phone down without saying a word. She knew the voice on the other end to be her unsuspecting mother, and she wasn't quite sure why she even called. She was just thankful Keon always had the caller id blocked on the house phone.

Keon kept one eye on the entrance going up to his apartment and the other on his phone he had resting on his knee below the steering wheel as he searched for any new text messages. Disappointed, he quickly dialed a sequence of numbers and placed his phone up to his ear, but the other party wasn't picking up as the call went straight to voicemail. He quickly called again only to receive the same results. Before he could dial the number once more, he saw

Ashley coming around the corner of their building, and he slid the phone into his pocket. She hopped in the car.

"What took you so long?" he asked.

"Stomach's a little upset."

"What the hell—you got butterflies?"

"No, but I'm good now."

He stared at her suspiciously. "Man, we ain't got all day and night to be spending at your moms. I know she's gonna want us to do that yuppie dinner thing she like does with company, but we're just gonna throw it all out there as fast as possible and wait for a response. Hopefully, it's quick so we can just get the hell on," he said.

"I understand, Keon."

"And oh yeah, I gotta make a quick stop before we get down that road."

"Where to?"

"Don't worry about all that. It's just a little business I gotta handle."

As he started the car, tears nearly formed in the wells of her eyes as she veered her gaze through the passenger's side window. She knew that the trip was destined to be one big waste of time. There would be a better chance of icicles forming in the most obscure reaches of Hell before the day she would witness her mother handing her one red cent for anything while she remained in a relationship with Keon. She hated the man and wasn't shy about making her feelings felt, but she was always respectful about it. She never went out and told Keon directly that she couldn't stand his guts, but he knew. Just like her mother knew Keon's feelings towards her were mutual.

It was a damned if you do and damned if you don't situation for Ashley. If she didn't agree to go down to her mother's house and ask her for the money, Keon was going to be mad and probably do his best to beat her brains out, and then when they arrived to her mother's house and she most certainly denied them any funds whatsoever, he was going to be even more irate and most likely beat her brains out when they returned home.

****

Keon eased into a parking space of an upscale apartment complex not too far from they're own. He shut the vehicle off, turned to Ashley and said, "I gotta check on this lead. I'll be right back."

She looked at him with a slight grin and didn't say a word. She knew exactly what he was there for and who he was there to see. Raven was her name, and she knew he was seeing her on the side for a little over a year now. She didn't care, though. As long as he was sneaking around with his side piece, he wasn't in her face trying to smash it in. As far as she was concerned, if his mistress really wanted him she could have him and all that went along with being his. She had just about her fill of the man.

As he jumped out of the car, she repositioned herself to get comfortable, and reclined in her spot, ready to get the entire day over with. Shortly after Keon disappeared into the walls of the apartment complex, her eyes fell on the passenger side mirror, noticing the same black car from the night before had slowly rolled up and briefly paused behind their vehicle. She quickly turned around in her chair, trying to stay snug behind the seat to see the passing car with her own eyes. Without a doubt, they were being followed.

Raven opened the door wearing a tight t-shirt that barely came down over her belly button and some pink jogging pants that fit snuggly around her perfectly round bottom. When she opened the door to Keon's smiling mug, she groaned and left him standing in the doorway.

"Damn, baby," Keon said as he walked in. "Nigga don't get a hug?"

"You think you deserve one?" she grunted as she walked to the sofa and plopped down on it.

"I'm just saying, a nigga ain't been through in a couple of days. It seems like you would miss a nigga or something."

She sucked her teeth and began flipping channels on the television set which was located on the other side of the room.

Keon was so uncomfortable by her cold reception when he walked up to the sofa, he chose not to sit. He said, "So, why your phone been off all day? Nigga been trying to call you and check in, but all I kept getting was your voicemail."

"Maybe that's all you deserve."

"What's all this talk about what a nigga deserve and shit?"

"You figure it out…playa."

"Oh, I guess you're all up in your feelings today." He dropped down on the other end of the plush leather chair and asked, "Man, you know I got some major shit on my plate right now. So what the hell a nigga do this time, Raven?"

She turned to him with the most disgusted stare and said, "Nigga, it ain't what you did. It's what you ain't doing?"

"And what's that?"

"You're a smart guy, you figure the shit out," she said as she threw the remote in his lap and stormed off towards the kitchen.

He shook his head and said under his breath, "This shit right here—never satisfied." He hopped up and made his way into the kitchen to join her. When he stepped in, she was at the counter slicing tomatoes. The sight of her with a knife made him feel slightly uneasy with the way she was acting.

"So where that chick at?" she asked not giving him any eye contact.

He let out a hard grunt and blurted out, "Shit, she out there in the car."

She dropped the knife and let out brief chuckle. "She's outside?"

"Yeah," he replied with a nod and goofy look on his face.

"So you brought her to my house?"

"No… no. Let's get the shit straight. I didn't bring her to your house. She's outside in the car. I gotta take her over to her momma house for something."

"They shole make some bold niggas these days, I tell ya." She laughed and returned to cutting her tomatoes. After a few seconds of intense tomato slicing, she dropped the knife again as her anger towards him became too unbearable for her to contain. She took a few moments to think about what he just revealed to her and said, "Let me ask you a question."

"Yeah."

"How in the hell does it even remotely seem like a good idea to bring another bitch to my house? I mean, what is it in your simple ass head that made you think bringing her over here was a good idea?

Please tell me now, Negro, because I'm beginning to think you're fuckin' retarded. I just wanna know."

"Damn, why you tryin' to handle me like that," he asked. "I mean, shit, you're the one not answering your phone and shit."

"It's because you're constantly doing stupid ass shit like this."

"Look, you weren't picking up your phone, and a nigga just got concerned—and right now a nigga is just trying to do his due diligence and check on your ass."

"Well, I'm fine, nigga. So now that you know that I'm fine, you can leave now and take your extra baggage on down the road with you," she said while pointing towards the exit.

"Awe girl, why you trying to be all hard and shit?" He eased up behind her and palmed her hips with both hands.

"Nah, don't touch me." She backed away from his lips as he attempted to kiss her on the side of her neck.

"You gonna let a nigga get a quickie while she out there waiting in the car? I'll straighten out that little attitude you tryin' to have."

She whipped around and tapped him on his lips and said, "Sorry, boo boo, but my little friend came early this month."

He chuckled, slowly slid his arms around her waist, and then pulled her into him. He said, "So, is it light or is it heavy?"

"Nigga," she said as she pushed him away by pounding both her knuckles into his chest. "You ain't getting up in me like that. I don't know what you're thinking."

"Awe, come on. It ain't like you ain't never did it like that before."

"Hell, even if I did, it ain't going down like that today," she said. "Go'on back down there and ask that bitch you brought over here that you got waiting on your stupid ass in the car to let you hunch on her while she's leaking blood."

"Awe, baby, why you gotta be like that," he asked while trying to grab the arm she was quickly pulling away from him.

"Cuz, Negro, I'm tired of being your side bitch!"

"Side bitch? Girl, come on, now. I done told you over and over again, you're my main lady. I ain't touched Ashley in over eight months."

"Yeah, nigga, you'll tell me anything," she folded her arms and issued him a disgusted frown.

"It's the truth!"

"Whatever!" she replied. "It shole look like I'm over here holding down the side bitch status while your ass is out there parading around Charlotte with her and going to family functions and shit. Boy, if you only knew how many niggas that just begged for the chance–just a sniff of it."

"What?" Keon barked.

"Nigga, I don't know what you getting all swole up for. You got the wrong bitch. Ain't none of that Mista-Miss Celie shit gonna fly over here with this bitch right ch'ere," she laughed. "You touch anything over here with force, and you gonna need a GPS tracker to find your fucking balls, nigga. Don't try and play me like that."

"Girl, whatever. Ain't nobody coming at you like that," he said as he pulled her close to him. "I'll never put my hands on you–not in a bad way—you my baby."

"And you never will, nigga. You best get that thought out your head if it ever find a way in it."

"Awe, girl, get up off that now," he replied. "Now look, so just to let you know, I'm taking her to her momma house so we can get this money."

"Money for what?"

"To pay back, Max."

"Pay back Max? I thought you said you handled that mess already."

"Nah, I said I was working on it. I ain't handle shit just yet."

"Boy!" she punched him on his shoulder. "And your ass rolling up over here knowing you still owe that nigga money!" She rushed to the small window over her sink to get a glance at the cars in the parking lot below.

"What the hell you getting all scared up for?"

"You owe a drug lord money, that's why, fool! You better stop playing with that dude."

"Man, fuck, Max! Everybody acting like that nigga don't breathe the same air and bleed blood the same way everybody else does. I told him we'll get him his money when we get it."

"Yeah, well if you don't get him that money, you gonna be one dead nigga. Don't try to play that role with me, I know ya'. You and your flunkies 'bout to be dead real quick if you don't get that man his money," she added, "And on that note, I'm sorry, Keon, but you gotta get the hell outta here with that mess." She positioned herself behind him and began pushing him down the hall towards the living room exit.

"So you just gonna turn your back on a nigga that quick?" he asked while mildly resisting her guidance towards the front room. "As much as I do for you—pay your rent, get your hair and nails done, buy you all kinds of shit that the next chick would love to have, and this is how you turn around and do a nigga? For real?"

She swung the front door open and said, "Get out your feelings, Keon. You can't do nothing for me dead," she rebutted. "That's exactly what you're gonna be if you don't straighten your mess out. I'm down for you and all, but I'm not trying to die for nobody. For real, you *gots* to go."

****

When Keon returned to the car, he did his best to conceal his frustration of being thrown out of the apartment by the women he considered to be his main chick. In front of Raven, he took her rejection in stride, but it pissed him off on the inside as he resented her for acting as if Max was more than the mere mortal that he saw him to be.

His gaze was straight forward as he slid his key in the ignition but froze before turning the switch. Ashley could tell something apparently didn't go his way. She didn't ask him how he was feeling because she really didn't care. She figured the love birds must've had a quarrel or something. She long suspected he didn't treat Raven like he treated her. Knowing him, she figured he probably worshipped the ground she walked on as she treated him like unadulterated crap in return. She assumed that's how it usually worked with a cheater and a beater like him.

"So I guess we gotta get on down the road."

"What?" he said as he finally snapped out of his spell.

"My mother's house. We probably should get moving."

He frowned, "Hell, I know that. I don't need you to be reminding me of nothin'. You just make sure you figure out a way to get that money we need. That's all the hell you need to be concerning yourself with." He started the car and began backing out of the parking space.

****

Ashley took deep, slow breaths as she could sense that a panic attack was coming on. They were parked outside of her mother's house, and Keon had already made his way out of the car as if they were at his own homecoming with his own family. She couldn't move. As her hands trembled, she found herself gawking at the two story brick house and its well kept shrubbery that wrapped around the residence as it had since she was a child. It was home, but she'd been away for so long she knew it wouldn't feel that way. She was reluctant to entertain all the questions that resided behind the brick walls that stretched before her.

Keon turned around towards the car once he realized she wasn't following him. To his displeasure, she hadn't even exited the car. A look of disdain sprawled across his face. "You gonna get the fuck out?" he asked as he swung his arms out.

The sight of his furious demeanor was an instantaneous fix to her nervousness. She quickly became less concerned about the mysteries that awaited her behind the walls of her mother's home and more cautious of the potential wrath of her chauffeur. Ashley took one final, deep breath, hopped out of the car and speedily joined him up the walkway to the front door.

"Don't fuck this up," he whispered to her.

Her mother, Rose, opened the door to them and a smile the size of Texas erupted across her face once she set eyes on her youngest daughter. "Ashley," she said as she slowly stepped out onto the porch and grabbed her daughter, embracing her tightly. "Oh, my child, my child, my child."

Her mother's excitement took her by surprise as Keon looked on with a smile followed by a brief nod. Rose's ecstatic response to seeing her daughter was exactly what he wanted to see. He could almost feel the money he needed to get from her gracing the palm of his hands.

"It's been so long, child. Too long," Rose exclaimed with watery eyes as she pulled away from Ashley. She scanned her over from head to toe, questioning herself about the reality of the moment. "I still can't believe you're standing here."

"I'm here, Momma," Ashley added, humbled by her mother's warm embrace.

The magic of the moment swiftly began to fizzle for Rose once she looked over to her daughter's companion. With a straight face, her only greeting to him was meek and uninspired, "Keon."

"Rose," he replied just as coldly as she spoke. It tickled him whenever he got the chance to see the displeasure of Ashley's family's faces when they saw him. He knew they couldn't stand him and that they yearned for the day that Ashley would leave him. He knew he would never let that happen because he felt that he owned her mind, body and soul, and he had no plans in ever letting her go. There wasn't a damn thing they could do about it.

Rose led the way into the home down the lavish hickory hardwood floors towards the dining room. "Your sisters are in the dining room already. Shall we join them?"

As Keon's eyes fell upon the luxurious oil paintings and exquisite décor that laced the walls of the foyer, he was not only reminded about how loaded Ashley's mother was, but he also recalled the original reason he wanted to make Ashley his in the first place. She was the little rich girl that was supposed to be his ticket out of the hood. His aspirations was for her to be the direct link to him and her parent's money. He just didn't factor in how critical her parents would be of their relationship when they discovered their precious darling had somehow managed to hook up with somebody from what they felt was the wrong side of town with a moderate criminal record they somehow used their money to dig up. It also didn't help that he was six years her senior.

Her father was so demanding that she leave him alone, he threw her out of the house and cut her out of his will right before he passed away. With him cutting her out of all that money, Ashley quickly went from being his prized blue chip stock to an inexperienced burden that essentially became his personal slave that was made to do whatever he requested, from cooking, cleaning and sex whenever he saw fit. If she disagreed with anything he positioned to her, he always had the remedy waiting for her in the form of his bare knuckles across her face and body, or his old school favorite, a strap across her backside. He wasted no time in letting her know that he was in charge when she found herself with nowhere else to go.

Draya and Shanice, Ashley's older, fraternal twin sisters sat at the end of the long dinner table and barely batted an eye to her as she greeted them. They were just too busy and transfixed in their own conversation to truly acknowledge her, but it was no surprise to Ashley. They were never close to her nor did they ever pay her any attention for the short time they all lived under the same roof. She wasn't certain if it was because of their differences in age, that being nine years, or if it was just that eerie twin bond she figured all twins had with each other.

It had been years since Ashley was graced by the aroma of her mother's succulent country cooking, and despite being on edge from the instance she arrived, she took a moment to take in the smells from the dishes that stretched across the table from end to end. She and Keon took the chairs opposite of Rose as they all sat in unison.

"Your brother should be arriving at any moment, so we'll give him a few minutes before we begin eating," said Rose as she sipped on a glass of wine she already had prepared prior to answering the door.

When Keon realized Ashley's younger brother, Dexter, would be joining them also, he immediately felt irritated. While Rose provided slight hints of her dislike for him in a subtle manner, Dexter made it no mystery that he couldn't stand him one bit, and he was always extremely vocal about it. Things were like that since the day he came over to inform Ashley about their Dad's passing, and she opened the door to him with a pair of black eyes. He didn't buy the story Keon instructed her to tell anyone asking about how she looked–that she'd been robbed and beaten at an ATM machine from some random street punk. Dexter had absolutely no doubt in his mind that her bruises were from Keon's hands as he aggressively made claims that he'd noticed marks and bruises on her before. Ever since that day, he had been begging for the chance to square off with Keon in a fair one. He just didn't know Keon was evenly eager to go one on one with him, also, just to teach the young, hot-head a lesson.

"So how have you been, Ashley?" Rose asked after a few moments of staring at her daughter. Her daughter's coyness wasn't sitting well with her as she remembered her child as always being a bit of a loner, but one that was confident and full of life.

Ashley didn't make any eye contact with her mother. Her vision was strictly focused on the wedding ring that was wrapped around her mother's finger. Her father told her so many stories about how hard he had to work to buy the symbol of love and commitment during her childhood. When she was young, she imagined she'd grow up and marry a dignified, hard working man like her father, but unfortunately she ended up with Keon—the exact opposite of him.

"Ashley?" her mother repeated. "Do you hear me speaking to you?"

Ripped out her of her daze by her mother's voice, she raised her head to her mother, then looked over to Keon, and then back to Rose. She was at a loss for words and didn't want to say the wrong thing. The mere anxiety of trying to figure out the right time and place she would ask her mother for the money she needed had her insides rumbling and her mind everywhere but at the dinner table.

"She's been doing alright, Rose," Keon answered.

After Keon's words, there was complete and utter silence. Ashley bowed her head. Her two sisters at the other end of the table ceased their conversation altogether and looked on to their mother, anxiously anticipating her response.

The old, bronze skinned lady raised her eyebrow at her daughter's companion and said, "I don't mean any harm, Keon, but I was talking to my daughter." She then turned her focus to Ashley. "I raised her to speak for herself as I did all my children, so I am confident she knows how to answer me when I'm speaking to her. Ashley–"

"I'm doing good, mom," she interjected before Keon could fix his mouth to say another word.

"I hear your mouth saying that you're good, but your posture tells me otherwise. To be frank, with all of this looking down, around and away, you almost look as if you're fearful of something," Rose looked Keon dead in his eyes. "Fearful in the one place you don't ever have to be fearful of anything or anyone–your home."

Keon let out a short grunt as his eyes crawled up the wall and onto the oil painting of Ashley's father that hovered over them and the dinner table. The portrait of the stern faced man made Keon feel even more uneasy as it almost appeared to him that the man was looking directly at him, straight from the grave. Keon contemplated if the trip was even worth it at all. His blood was beginning to boil from the elevated tension in the room. He thought if they could get through the visit and obtain the money he needed, they would never have to see his black ass again. Unless, of course, Rose kicked the bucket and left his old lady with the money–that would definitely be the next and final time they'd see his black ass again.

"What the hell is he doing here?" Dexter yelled out as he dashed towards Keon. All the young man could see was red the moment he entered the dining room and laid eyes on the man he'd been yearning to square up with for past few years. Keon quickly jumped up and backed away from the table, sending his chair flying to the floor while clinching his fists, anxiously waiting to defend himself.

"Dexter!" Rose yelled as she and her twin daughters rushed towards him to prevent him from connecting with his first swing at Keon.

"You better back up, son." Keon warned him as he continued to back away from the muscular young man. "Ain't nobody come here to be fighting nobody."

"Well that makes one of us," said Dexter while attempting to escape the tugs and restraints of his family.

"Dexter! Dexter!" yelled Rose as she worked herself in front of him while pushing him backwards towards his sisters who managed to finally get a secure hold of his arms. "Settle down, son! You settle down right this minute."

"Nah, Ma," Dexter replied. "Ain't nobody stupid. We know what he does to her. I've seen his handy work with my own damn eyes. He beats her. He beats the hell out of her."

"Dexter, you watch your mouth in my house and cut out all of this foolishness right this minute," Rose demanded while wagging her finger in her son's face. "I didn't raise any hoodlums in this house, now cut it out, I say."

"You know what, let's be real for the first time since I got here" said Keon. "I ain't family. We all know that. There's no reason for me to even be up in here trying to impose. This is yall's time together.

I'm 'bout to go outside and let y'all do y'all family thang. I didn't come here to stir no trouble."

"You damn right you ain't family," Dexter said.

"Dexter!" Rose called to him with a firm look.

"I'm sorry, Ma," he replied, still angry but no longer requiring his older sisters to restrain him.

"Keon," said Rose, "You don't have to leave. Despite our differences, you are a guest in this house, and I made enough food for everyone."

"Nah, Rose, I insist," Keon replied.

"Nobody begging him to stay," said Dexter.

"Dexter, that's enough," said Rose.

Ashley never moved a muscle as she kept her seat and looked straight ahead as if there wasn't any commotion at all in the home. Keon leaned into Ashley's ear and whispered, "You make sure you talk her into giving you that money or his ass whoppin' belongs to you." He kissed her on her cheek. "I'll see you in a few, babe." He added loudly, just for put-on purposes for the rest of the family.

She nodded as he looked to the rest of the family and said with a short wave, "Folks. I'll see myself out."

They watched silently as he retreated from the dining room.

"Momma, we got to go, too," said Draya.

"Already?" Rose asked with a surprised look on her face. "We're finally all in one place, together as a family. We haven't been like this since before your father passed away."

"I know, Momma, but Draya's right, we gotta go," Shanice added. "We're running inventory tomorrow night and nobody's trying to be in that store past midnight like the last time."

"I know that's right," Draya added. "We can't leave those types of responsibilities to the help. Their slack behinds will have us all over budget."

"Well, I know you girls stay busy with your boutiques and all, but you can't leave until I make you both a plate."

"Girl, we didn't say we were leaving without taking a plate of your food, Momma," Shanice laughed while giving her twin a high five.

"Amen," Draya added with a brief chuckle.

"Well, you come on here and follow me to this here kitchen," said Rose. "Dexter, Ashley, I'll be right back." She led them into the kitchen as Dexter took a seat at the table across from Ashley.

"That's cool, Ma," Dexter replied.

"Nice seeing you again, Ash," said Draya as she bent over to give her sister a short, cutesy hug that barely included any actual touching.

Dexter grabbed a roll from the bread basket, took a huge bite from it and watched his sister look away and around at everything in the dining room but him. He said, "So why'd you bring that filth up in here? You for one, should know he's not welcome here–ever!"

"Look, Dexter, I know what you're going to say, and you're wrong. Keon doesn't hit me," Ashley said, almost in disbelief she could put those lying words together and allow them to escape from her own lips. "I've told you this over and over again. You should stop spreading this mess around the family."

"My ass," Dexter replied. "How you gonna bring that clown up in Momma's house, knowing good and well she can't stand him? We all know how he treats you? You're nothing but his punching bag. He doesn't love you, and you know it. I didn't dream up them black eyes I saw on you nor the bruises on your arms. I know what the hell I saw."

"Dexter, whatever goes on in my house, I can handle."

"Yeah, right," he shook his head while frowning at the sight of her. He couldn't believe she was so loyal to such a lowlife. It sickened him down to his stomach. "Dude is beneath you. He never deserved you, and somehow you can't even see that. To hell with what everybody keeps trying to tell you."

Her brother's words cut deep but not because he was saying them so bluntly and without any regard, but because all of his words were true. She couldn't even keep a straight face and try to pretend she wasn't going through hell every day she lived under the same roof with Keon.

There wasn't anything she wanted more than to send Keon on his way without her, but in her heart she knew it wasn't an option. She feared for her brother's life and the rest of the family with what Keon might do to them and her if she left him. Dexter was a hot head and even trained to fight by way of Taekwondo, but he wasn't a street dude like Keon. Keon was tough enough to take a well-deserved beating, but he'd be sure to come back and sneak you and take you out another day. She understood that all of the special training and fighting in the world could never prepare him for someone like Keon—not his kind of evil. If he couldn't get you face to face, he'd still get you—one way or another.

"I mean, what happened to you," Dexter asked, with an disgusted expression. "You were the one that taught me how to stand up for myself when we were growing up. Now look at you."

She remained silent as her mother reentered the dining room. "Okay, well the girls are squared away and on their way home," said Rose as she took a seat next to her son. "I guess that just leaves us three with some good eating and some overdue catching up."

"I've done my share of catching up for one night, Ma." Dexter proclaimed as he rose from the table, his concentration on his sister unbroken.

Rose turned to her son with her mouth open and her hands out. She said, "Wait a minute, you haven't even eaten anything."

"You know what, Ma, I'm not even hungry."

"But, Dexter," she said.

"I need to shower," he said as he stormed out of the room.

Rose didn't even try to stop him as she finally threw in the towel on the disaster of a dinner. She shook her head and took another sip of her wine, while wishing she had poured herself something a little stronger if she'd known the night was going to turn out the way it had.

"Well, Ashley, I guess we need to start eating as much of this food as we can so it won't go to waste," Rose said while scooping up a spoon of green beans and dropping them onto her plate.

"I'm not really hungry, either, Momma."

Rose let out a tiring sigh, "Well, I'm not really surprised child. Seems like no one came to dinner to actually eat dinner tonight."

"Momma, Keon and I came over to ask for a loan," she blurted out. It seemed like the longer she waited to bring it up, the worst the night got. She just couldn't keep thinking about the different ways to position it any longer and decided just to let it out raw and ugly.

"Really," she said while dropping her utensils beside her plate as she took a few moments to digest her daughter's revelation.

"Yes, mam," she answered while looking down at her own reflection in her empty dinner plate. "We wanted to put a decent down payment on a home we just fell in love with once we saw it. One that we could perhaps even start a family in," she lied. The words that came out of her mouth made her feel like the lowest scum on the earth. She just hated lying to her mother, especially in the form of the bull she was sifting out by portraying a happy and promising future with Keon.

Rose's eyes hadn't left her daughter since the moment she asked for the money. She wondered what was going on in her daughter's head. The woman before her looked like her Ashley, but she was far from the young lady that she'd remember raising. "Well, I guess we need to mosey on down to your father's office and find my check book."

Ashley eyes shot opened as she thought her ears had deceived her. "Huh?"

"Well, come on." Her mother eased up from the table and said, "Let's get to it."

Ashley rose from her chair and began to cautiously follow her mother out of the dining room and down the hall. She felt relieved she had finally coached herself into asking her mother for the cash, but she was also suspicious of mother's willingness to oblige. She didn't even ask how much she needed. Although her mother had plenty money, it just didn't feel right for her not to ask how much money she was actually requesting from her. Nevertheless, she was mere moments away from getting the finances she needed to get Keon off her back, and she just couldn't believe it. She felt like pinching herself to make sure she was awake.

Keon sat on the back of his car blowing smoke circles in the air as he waited for a text response from Porkchop. After a few moments without a reply he flicked his cigarette to the ground and dialed Porkchop's number. To his surprise, his ally's phone went straight to voicemail. Infuriated, he spoke into the phone once prompted by the voicemail box, "Aye man, what the fuck? You suppose to hit me back with the word on that bitch nigga, and I ain't hear shit from you all day. I hope your punk ass didn't leave town. If you did, you know you're on some fuckboy shit, for real. But I know you know better than that, so hit me back when you get this message. Don't disappoint a nigga." He ended the call and mumbled, "Shit!" He looked towards the house and said, "Girl, you better come through for a nigga."

When Ashley followed her mother into her father's office, a frightening streak of nervousness came over her. The last time she was in her father's office her, old man was alive, kicking and determined to sculpt his children's lives the way he saw best fit. It was in this very room that he gave her his final ultimatum to leave Keon or be banished from his house forever. He explained to her that he didn't want to see her again if she wasn't going to abide by his wishes of leaving the overgrown career criminal, whom at the time was everything she thought she wanted in a man. Leave him or he wanted no part of her in his life, he told her. It was all a pile of regrets now, and although she was mad as hell at her father for trying to force her into choosing between him and Keon, she finally realized he was only looking at the man she loved without the infatuated eyes she couldn't take off of him. It was now that she wished she'd listened to her father as she lived most days regretting not being able to tell the stubborn old man that she was sorry and he was actually right.

"Have a seat," her mother stated as she walked around her deceased husband's cherry oak desk and pointed to the chair across from it, signaling Ashley to sit.

"No, I'd rather stand, Momma."

Rose grinned, "You're gonna ask me for money and not adhere to at least one of my requests?"

Ashley begrudgingly sat in the chair. The chills just wouldn't stop flaring up across her arms and down her spine. She sat in the spot where her father leaned against the desk before her and pleaded for her to not walk out on the family–to use her head and not her foolish heart. It was his last request to her, the final day she saw him alive. The guilt was agonizing. Her heart raced as mounds of grief weighed down on her soul as she thought that if she only had listened to him, things would've turned out much differently. She couldn't help but think that somehow he could've lived a little longer if she only obeyed him and broke away from the man he warned would bring her so much pain and heartache. He was so right about Keon.

"Did you hear me child?" Rose asked.

"What's that?" asked Ashley.

"You didn't hear a word I just said, did you?" Rose said while shaking her head. "I asked how much money do you need."

Apprehensive, she asked, "You're not going to ask me about where the house is located, or how it looks?"

"Why should I? You said that you and Keon loved the place."

"And you're just going to write us out this check and not even ask when we'll be able to pay it back?"

"Sure," she said as she pulled out her checkbook from the drawer on the side of the desk and sat it on the table. She uncapped her ballpoint pen and asked, "Now how much do you need?"

"Well, we need eighty thousand dollars, Ma. We should be able–"

"That's fine. Don't even worry about paying it back." Rose began filling out the check.

"Are you serious, Momma?"

"Absolutely."

Ashley couldn't believe it. It was almost too good to be true. She watched her mother carefully as she wrote the check out. After her mother graced the paper with her signature, she slid it across the cherry oak desk.

Before Ashley could pick it up and grab it, Rose said, "This check is yours under one condition."

Ashley took a step back and sat back down on the edge of her chair. She replied, "And what's that mother?"

"I will give you this money and you won't ever have to worry about paying me back if you take this here check, walk it out to that man outside and tell him this is his to keep as long as he leaves this home without you and call this so-called relationship you have with him over–for good!"

Ashley quickly realized her mother was determined to finish what her father wasn't able to complete. She knew her mother's urgency to write her out a check was just too good to be true. The craziest thing about it was there wasn't anything in the world she wanted more than to be rid of the man she despised so much. There just wasn't a way he'd let her go that easy–not without a fight and not without someone dying. It just wasn't going to happen without some type of tragedy, and it didn't matter what dollar amount was thrown at him

"Momma, I know this may be difficult for you, but you gotta respect..."

"Respect what? Your relationship, Ashley?" She rose from her deceased husband's executive leather chair and leaned over his desk with both her hands planted on top of it. "You don't think I know that man out there abuses you? That he puts his filthy, stinking hands on a child of mine–a child that I raised? Every time I see that man, it takes the unrelenting strength of the Lord to keep me from killing his black ass."

"Mom..."

"Don't Mom me," she wagged her finger towards her daughter. "Don't you do it. Don't you dare do it," she yelled. "That man got you in here acting like a shell of yourself. I don't even recognize my own child anymore with all of this looking down and around and everywhere except for in the eyes of the person that's speaking to you. I didn't raise you like that. I didn't raise any of my children like that. You're better than this, Ashley. You're better."

"Momma, we need this money."

"And you can have it—ever last cent. You can have it all. But in order to get it, you have to agree to my terms."

Ashley was stunned. She rose from her chair, fighting back tears. Once she looked into her mother's eyes, she couldn't hold them back anymore and nor could Rose. They both stood still with tears streaming down their faces, stubborn in their own separate ways.

"I'm giving you an out, Ashley. That's all I'm trying to do. I know his type. I've known it all my life. There is no good in that man out there. He will drag you down into the depths of hell with him if he can—further down than he's already taken you."

"You don't understand, Momma," she cried, while shaking her head. "You guys don't ever seem to understand." She yearned to take her up on her offer, but no figure she wrote down on that check would be enough to recapture her freedom from Keon.

"Oh I understand, child. More that you could ever imagine." Rose picked the check up and held it before her daughter. "Take this money to him and get your life back. End it while you can."

****

When Keon noticed Ashley approaching the car, he put away his phone and sat from his reclined position in the driver's seat. The expression on her face didn't appear to be a pleasant one, but he hadn't seen her smile in quite some time so that was nothing new to him. He really didn't care how she was feeling as his only concern was if she had come through for him or not, and he was certain she did. She surely understood the agony that awaited her if she failed him.

Ashley hopped in the car with her nerves shot and chest feeling as if it could explode. She could feel Keon eyes on her as she bowed her head, let out a deep sigh and said, "She didn't give us the money."

"Wha...Really."

She looked at him and gave him a bit of a nod and said, "Yes." She knew she was in deep trouble. She was just hoping he'd have enough decency to drive out of her mother's yard before he started his rampage.

He looked at her with a hopeless expression as he couldn't believe his ears. She came back empty handed. Plan A through Z for him had fallen apart. He wanted to call her every foul name in the book, but the shock of her coming back empty handed made him choke back his words. She had to be kidding him. As he gazed at her with her hanging head, he was hoping she'd raise her head and tell him she was only kidding, but she didn't. He could tell by her tense demeanor she was waiting for him to go ape crazy, but he didn't. He simply said, to her surprise and his, "Well, I guess you tried."

There was a deadening silence in the car for a few moments as he just sat there gazing at her mother's house, still in disbelief, contemplating requesting the money himself. She looked towards him but not in his face, only towards his knee where his tightened fist sat idly. He started the car and backed out of the driveway. As they moved down the road, she remained terrified to look at him. She thought he would've gone ballistic once he got about a mile from her mother's residence, but he was still calm–too calm.

The further away they travelled from her mother's home, the more relaxed she started to feel. She thought maybe he was just trying to scare her up to force her to be more inclined to ask her mother for the money he needed. She figured he had to have known the odds of her mother just giving them the money in the first place weren't good due to the fact that she was practically exiled from the family for years, and the only reason for it was for being with him.

After driving about five miles down the barren stretch of road, Keon slammed on the car brakes and quickly jabbed an unsuspecting Ashley square on her chin, forcefully propelling the side of her head against the passenger side window. He put the car in park in the middle of the road and yelled, "What the hell you got me way down this road wasting my fucking time for?"

"Keon, I.." she attempted to explain, but Keon struck her across the bridge of her nose with the back of his hand.

"Bitch, don't try to explain shit to me," he said. "You understand me?" When she didn't immediately respond, he held his hand near her face at striking distance. "I asked you if you understood my ass, heffa?" He lowered his hand once she tearfully acknowledged him by nodding her head.

Tears raced down her cheeks as she regained her composure from the brief dizziness she sustained from his strikes. She rubbed her chin as he continued on with his rant. She didn't look at him, fearing he'd hit her again out of his own paranoia, believing that she was looking at him in a disrespectful way.

"I told your ass you was gonna pay if you didn't come through for me with this money," he angrily professed. "Got your brother in my goddamn face talking all this cold cash trash, like he can beat my ass. Boy is your ass gonna pay when we get back to the crib. Your sorry ass had just one goddamn thing to do. Just one goddamn thing to do, and you couldn't even do that shit right. You're a goddamn disappointment. I don't know what the fuck I'd ever seen in your lousy ass."

"Keon, I tried."

He chopped her across her forehead with the side of his hand and said, "Don't you talk back to me woman!"

As the tears flowed she simply nodded, trying her earnest not to break down completely.

"You know I'll fuck you up out here on this road. Don't you tempt me," he warned her while pointing at her forehead. "I told you what was gonna happen before we even got down here so you may as well get ready for what's coming to your ass. And I know your ass didn't really wanna get me that money because you would've gotten it. I ain't crazy. You just ain't good for a goddamn thing!" He slung the car in drive and began barrelling down the road again, his expression embodied with rage. "Can't do shit I tell you. You're worthless. You're fucking worthless. Good for shit."

He went on and on until she didn't even hear his hurtful words anymore. She was numb to it. She only wished she was numb to his physical attacks. She also wondered if she should've just taken her mother up on the offer and bring him the check in exchange for her freedom from him.

****

Keon didn't yield his onslaught of derogatory words towards Ashley since he attacked her a few miles down from her mother's house. His only shift in focus was when his stomach started grumbling because he hadn't eaten anything all day. He got mad at her for that, too. He ripped into her for not thinking enough of him to bring him a plate out, knowing good and well she failed at getting him his money.

He backed his car into a parking space facing the side entrance of his favorite hood restaurant, Biggie Burgers. "You go in there and get me a Biggie Max Burger with cheese. Tell them I don't want no mayonnaise on my shit. If they put mayonnaise on my shit, I'm already warning you–I'm not gonna be a happy camper so you best stress that shit to them inside." He slapped a twenty in the palm of her hand and warned, "If a nigga try to holla at you in there, you better act like the mother fucker don't exist. You got me?"

She nodded and slowly eased out of the car. Her ribs were sore and it pained her if her arm merely rubbed up against them. Slowly walking towards the entrance, she instantly became nauseous from the burnt grease smell that always exuded from the former McDonalds building rebranded with graffiti that embellished the Biggie Burger moniker on every wall that kept the deteriorating structure standing. She wondered how he could even eat out of such a place as the outside of the building was in need of a severe litter pickup, and the inside was normally no better.

He watched her slowly walk into the building. Once she entered the restaurant, he slid his phone out of his pocket. He was disappointed when he realized he didn't receive a single text message or missed call from neither Porkchop nor Raven. Right before he could dial his side chick to get on her case for not checking on him, there was a hard knock against his window.

He immediately hurled over towards the passenger side of the car, fearful that he was about be under attack from one of Max's men. "What the…" He looked towards his window to a sparingly dressed woman standing just outside of his car. He felt a sigh of relief, but he quickly rolled the window down halfway to angrily ask her, "Fuck you want?"

"Hey, handsome," she replied with a smile that didn't include any front or bottom teeth, just brownish fangs hanging from the corners of her mouth. "I can make your dreams come true for fifteen dollars."

He looked the filthy woman from head to toe, thinking at best she was probably a six or a seven during her good years, but she was far from it today. "Bitch, I'll pass," he replied.

"Well, fuck you then, faggot!" she yelled. She then pressed on away from his car. He just shook his head, without any aspirations to bother with wasting a response on the woman as he rolled his window back up.

Before she could make it into the restaurant, a car stopped right in front of Keon's. The driver tapped on his horn a couple of times in an attempt to get the woman's attention. She halted, smiled and jogged over to the driver's window. She bent over into his window after looking around the immediate area to see if anyone was paying them any attention. After exchanging a few words with the driver, she glided over to the passenger side door and jumped in. The car sped off.

Keon thought the driver of the vehicle must've been mighty hard up for a trick. "Niggas." As he chuckled to himself, he noticed a young man wearing headphones, and bobbing his head, while sitting on a couple of crates alongside the wall on the backside of the restaurant. He then noticed Ashley approaching the car with his food. He looked over to the man and then back at Ashley. He had an idea, but he wasn't sure how much it would benefit him.

Ashley jumped into the car and handed him his food. "I made sure they didn't add any mayonnaise, and they made the burger fresh just how you like it."

He snatched the bag from her with the wheels still turning in his head. Looking into the bag, he grabbed the burger, checked it to see if it had any mayonnaise on it and then took a big chomp out of it. His eyes then returned to the guy sitting on the crates.

Ashley bowed her head as she waited for him to finish his meal so he could drive them home and begin her punishment. The sooner he was able to do whatever he was going to do, the sooner he could leave for the night and be with his other woman.

He took a swallow from his drink and pointed towards the guy on the crates. "I want you to walk up to that nigga right there and tell him you'll give him head for forty dollars?"

"What?" Her head quickly popped up, alarmed and shocked by his request. "Huh?"

"Bitch, what'cha looking at that nigga for?" He back-handed her across the bridge of her nose with the same hand he was holding his drink, spilling the beverage all over her chest and lap. "Fuck you pop your head up so fast for? You wanna do it or something, bitch?"

"No, Keon, I didn't even know what you were talking about," she cried.

"Bitch, you been out here playing me? You been having some nigga in my crib with you while I'm out here hustlin' in these here streets?" His eyes were almost bulging out of his head as Ashley attempted to explain herself.

"No, Keon, no… I was just trying to understand what you were asking of me."

"Bitch, you lying," he said as he smacked her across her lips.

Blood immediately began to trickle down from the corner of her mouth as she held her hands up in an attempt to block his barrage of jabs. She screamed and pleaded for him to stop as she tried to deter his punches. When she successfully blocked her face from getting hit, he would then direct his punches towards her midsection.

"You wanna give that nigga some head, don't ya? I knew I couldn't trust your scandalous ass."

"No, Keon. Stop! Stop hitting me," she begged him.

"Stupid, bitch," he yelled as he poured on his vicious bombardment of strikes. He struck her as hard as he could from his side angle, furious with himself because his punches weren't more on target.

"Keon, stop it, please!"

One of his jabs slipped through her guard and plowed her face against her window. There was silence as her hands fell to her lap, and her body went limp. When he realized she wasn't moving, he held off on his punishment and began examining her. "Ashley?"

Silence.

He looked her idle body over and a slight stroke of fear overcame him. With her head lying against the passenger window, he thought he might've killed her. He repositioned himself in his chair, not believing he actually struck her hard enough to really kill her. He then picked his burger up from his lap and bit another chunk from it—his angry eyes still piercing through her. "Girl, stop all that damn playing and get your ass up."

She didn't utter a word nor did she move an inch. Her silence infuriated him.

"Alright, then, just lay your stupid ass there. Play dead. I like it quiet in this bitch while I'm driving anyway," he said as he stuck his key into the ignition. There still wasn't any movement from her as he faced her again, now even more irritated that she wasn't responding to him. "Ash," he called as he nudged her shoulder. "Stop fuckin' playing and get the hell up… Ashley! Now that black out shit is getting played," he pushed her again, this time more forceful. Her limp body fell forward and the collision of her head against the dashboard sounded off an unnerving thud. When he noticed the stream of blood coming from the side of her head, it alarmed him, "Girl, what the fuck?"

He pushed her upright and began to softly pat her on her cheek. "Ashley… Ashley… Wake your dumb ass up. Ashley…"

****

Darkness.

"I knew he was gonna do it to you, child. I knew it."

"Momma," Ashley called out to her mother's voice. She couldn't see a thing as she was surrounded by darkness. She couldn't even see her own body. All she could feel was the coldness against her body from wherever she blindly stood. She could hear light whispers surrounding her as the voices intertwined themselves with the darkness. "Girl, why'd you let him do this to you?" she heard the hurt in her mother's strained voice. "I told you he was gonna do this to you!"

"Momma, what he do? Where are you," she asked frantically. "I can't see anything. Where am I? What happened, Momma? What happened to me?"

"That mother fucker," was the sound of her brother, Dexter's voice.

"Dexter?"

"You let that bastard put you here, Ashley. Nobody could tell you nothing," said Dexter. "That mother fucker!"

"Dexter, tell me what's going on, please," she cried. "It's so dark, so cold. Please tell me I'm not…"

"You stupid, bitch!" It was Keon's voice.

Fear overcame her at the sound of his voice. She couldn't utter a word. She didn't know where she was, but she figured he put her there.

"You had to fuck things up again. I didn't even hit your stupid ass that damn hard. You don't have to play dead, bitch. I can turn your fantasies into a reality. Come here!" She could feel again, the feeling of his hands clasping around her neck. "This time you die."

"Noooo!" She bolted up from the bed. Her eyes shot open as she was awakened to see a nurse standing at the foot of her bed holding a tablet with a stunned expression. She was lying in bed at the hospital.

"You're awake," said the nurse. "That's great. I'll get Dr. Ramirez."

"Wait! What happened?" she asked as she stroked the top of her head to fell a bandage plastered just above her eyebrow.

"You were in an accident," said the nurse.

"I was?"

"Yes mam," the nurse answered in a deep southern voice as she nodded. "You bumped your head pretty hard. You had your husband quite terrified when he brought you in."

"My hu..." she stopped herself. She was trying to put the events leading up to her lost of consciousness together as best as she could, but her splitting headache wasn't giving her any relief whatsoever. She slowly eased backwards onto her pillow and began caressing the spot of her forehead that was bandaged. "How long was I out?"

"Just a few hours, hun."

"Oh," she answered as a sharp stroke of pain moved through her head. "Mam, please tell me you have some type of pain reliever."

"I'll get something for that headache of yours in a few shakes. Why I know the pain has to be excruciating. By the way, what's a smart young lady like you doing riding around without wearing a seatbelt anyhow?"

She figured that must've been the cause of her injuries according to Keon, his explanation to the hospital—some type of a car accident. She just shrugged her shoulders to the old nurse, not disputing anything she'd been told. Ashley began to recall the flurry of punches Keon threw at her before smashing her skull into the window, and she couldn't remember anything else after that. She expected him to try to harm her some kind of way because she couldn't provide him with what he wanted, but that didn't make what he did right.

"Here you go, sweetheart." The nursed handed her two aspirins and a small cup of water. "I'm heading off to notify Dr. Ramirez that you've finally awakened from your slumber."

Keon laid back in a chair located in the small lobby with his clothes wrinkled from several hours of trying to position himself comfortable. He was nodding in and out of consciousness until he caught a glimpse of Dr. Ramirez pacing down the aisle, almost passing him by. He quickly hopped out of his seat and began tucking his shirt into his pants as he yelled, "Doc! Doc, did she wake up yet?"

Dr. Ramirez quickly ceased her stride and spun around. "You are?" the middle aged Puerto Rican woman with shoulder length graying brown hair asked as she looked through her tablet.

"Keon... Keon Robinson."

"Oh, yes, Mr. Robinson. You and ahhh— your wife were in that car accident last night."

"Yeah," he answered with a nervous grin."

"I haven't received any further updates about Ms. Parker's status, but when I do you will be notified. Oh, and there's no restriction on visitation. You could sit in the room with her. The chairs are far more comfortable."

"Nah, nah, I don't like to see her like that," he nodded.

"Her injuries weren't too severe," Doctor Ramirez added. "Some bumps and bruises and a mild concussion."

"Yeah, I always tell her about wearing that damn seatbelt. She don't ever listen, though. And then some asshole came right out of nowhere—almost sideswiped the shit out of us, doc."

"Hmmm," she looked over her tablet. "With the injuries she sustained, it's amazing she didn't fly through the windshield—with her not wearing her seatbelt and all."

"Yeah, you're right, doc," Keon agreed with a bit of a frown. He was suspicious the doctor was letting on to something else. There was a brief, uncomfortable pause between the two.

"Well, I've reached out to Ms. Parker's family to notify them that she's here."

"What the hell did you do that for, Doc? I'm her family."

"Well, we couldn't locate you on any of Ms. Parker's files as a point of contact even though you claimed to be married."

"Common law, Doc, you know that's still a thing around these parts."

"Not so much in this state, Mr. Robinson. Besides, legally we have to follow hospital protocol." She took a deep breath and added, "And with all due respect Mr. Robinson, I do have my reservations about the entire incident."

"Reservations?" Keon said, "About the incident? What? You calling me a liar, Doc?"

"No, Mr. Robinson, I'm not making any accusations whatsoever. I just have my reservations. Now, if you'd prefer that I notify the authorities to discuss the details of the incident instead of the family members Ms. Parker has listed on file, I could oblige."

"Nah, Doc, you've done enough." Keon said.

"Alrighty." The doctor shrugged her shoulders then walked off.

Before Dr. Ramirez could get two steps away from Keon, she was approached by Ashley's nurse.

Keon overheard the nurse advising the doctor that Ashley had awaken, and Dr. Ramirez swiftly followed the nurse to Ashley's room. This worried him because he was unsure if Ashley was going to go along with his story or not. He had enough problems to concern himself with than to be worrying about some cops questioning him about some type of domestic assault. He knew Ashley wasn't crazy enough to rat him out, but he wasn't one hundred percent sure of her loyalty after the way he mangled her around in the car.

As he stood in the hall, his eyes didn't leave Ashley's room door. When Dr. Ramirez finally exited the room with the nurse, he hustled back into the lobby until they left the area. He, then, walked down to her room door, stormed in and rushed to her bed, "Alright, what did you tell that fucking wetback, doctor?"

"I didn't tell her anything," Ashley nervously answered, startled by his chaotic entrance.

"Um hmm, um hmm," he pointed towards her and in a lowered but commanding tone he said, "When your damn momma come up here, you better tell her you weren't wearing your damn seatbelt. It ain't gonna be a good thing if they come running up in my face today. I won't hold shit back on their asses."

"Who called momma?" she asked.

"Your damn doctor did, that's who!"

"Why?"

"I don't fuckin' know. She just did," he said, "With her nosey ass. You sure you didn't elaborate on anything with that woman?"

"No, I didn't. I just went along with what the nurse said you told them."

Keon nodded as he raked his fingers through his hair, still uptight, but slowly calming down. He walked over to the window and gazed down at the parking lot. The sky was dark orange from the rising sun.

"I ain't got no time for no extra shit. You passing out in that car set me back some serious time. Time I needed to fix this shit."

She took a deep sigh and lowered her head, not saying a word. She simply listened as he blamed all his misfortunes on her.

"It fucking looks like Porkchop done skipped town on a nigga," he said as he whipped around to face her. He threw his hands up in the air and added, "After all the shit I've done for that nigga—all the shit I've done for his ass. He was the last nigga I ever thought would do me like this."

"He hasn't called you?"

"Are you listening to any fucking thing I'm saying," he replied. "No. Hell no, he ain't called me—that motherfucker! I told him I had a fucking plan, but no, this nigga done went dark—his black ass."

There was a knock at the door. It captured their attention as the door sprang opened and Rose eased in. However, complete chaos broke out as Dexter zipped right in from behind his mother and yelled, "You!" His gaze was set on Keon as he dashed across the room and nailed Keon with a right jab that forced them both onto the floor. The two began to tussle as Dexter fought like a man possessed. Rose and Ashley both screamed for the two to stop battling as a couple of male nurses rushed into the room to separate the men.

"You son of a bitch," yelled Dexter as he was forced towards the entrance by one of the nurses.

"Rose, you better get that boy of yours," Keon said as he wiped a splattering of blood from the corner of his lips. He was totally out of breath as the young man was a little too much to handle than he originally imagined.

"Knock it off, Dexter" Rose demanded.

All Ashley could do was watch from her bed. She was happy to see her brother get the best of Keon, but she didn't want him to get hurt or sent to jail.

One of the nurses yelled, "Okay, you both are gonna have to leave the premises. This is a hospital not a wrestling arena."

"Oh he can stay," Keon said as he walked towards the door. He casted an angry glance at Ashley and added, "I'm going downstairs to get into my car. I'm leaving in thirty minutes."

Ashley didn't say a word but bowed her head when her mother faced her with a stern look as she waited for her to respond to Keon, however there wasn't a response.

"Tough guy," Keon looked towards Dexter. "We'll get up. We'll get up."

"Anytime, Negro, anytime," Dexter answered repeatedly nodding, anxious to get his hands on him again.

"Chill out, dude," said the nurse as he pushed Dexter backwards a bit to allow Keon to walk by to prevent the two from tangling again.

"I got plenty more helpings for you—believe that," Dexter emphasized.

Keon responded with a chuckle as he slowly exited the room. The staff that had entered the room to control the ruckus exited behind him. Dexter was so upset he punched into wall.

"If you want to go run behind him, you won't be getting an escort from me," said Rose.

"What are you talking about, Ma?"

"A car accident, Ashley, really?" she said. "We passed right by his car on the way in, and there was no damage on that car that wasn't there already. What kind of a fool do you take us for? And to make matters worse, that man didn't have a mark on him until Dexter put hands on him."

"Ma, I got hurt by him trying to avoid the accident," she lied while shaking her head closing her eyes, already fed up with discussing the situation. "I wasn't wearing my seatbelt, Ma."

"Oh my flippin' God," Dexter barked. "This crap is useless with her, Ma. She's protecting this clown once again. She's doing it again."

"Dexter, please," begged Ashley.

"Look, I'm out of here." He pointed at her and warned, "You can let that clown beat your goddamn brains out if you want to—I'm done with it."

"Dexter!" Rose interjected.

"What, Ma? Why should we care? She doesn't." He slammed the door shut behind himself, angrily leaving the room.

Their focus rested on the door that Dexter had just stormed through. Neither knew what to say to each other, but they both had a lot churning on the inside. They just didn't know how to say it. Ashley wanted to reassure her younger brother and her mother that she had everything under control, despite the fact that she really didn't. Rose, simply wanted peace and happiness for all her children, and she wanted to demand Ashley stay away from Keon as long as eternity.

Rose sat on the edge of her daughter's bed. "He put you on the clock. What are you going to do child?"

There wasn't an immediate response from Ashley as the room stood awkwardly silent for a couple minutes. Rose's attention never left her daughter, despite Ashley never looking back at her. Instead, her focus just bounced from the edge of the bed and from wall to wall during the silence.

"I gotta do what I have to do, Ma," Ashley finally responded as she began to ease out of the bed.

"Child, where are you going?"

"I'm about to catch Keon before he leaves," she said as she walked towards the chair, grabbed her jeans, and slid them on.

"What?" Rose hopped off of the bed and moved towards her. "After all of this, you're really considering leaving with this man?"

"After all of what, Ma?" Ashley asked. She looked directly at her mother and explained, "He didn't touch me. I know it seems hard for you to believe, but the story is true."

"And you expect me to believe that?"

"You have no choice."

Her mother had no answers as she helplessly watched Ashley slip on her shirt and gingerly creep towards the door. Suddenly, she stopped. "I told you back at the house before I left, I got this, Ma."

"Ashley, don't…" Before she could complete her sentence, Ashley left the room. Tears began to roll down her cheeks because once again, she wasn't sure if she'd ever see her daughter living and breathing again. It infuriated her to be so helpless, but she knew her daughter to be bullheaded just like her father was. She was destined to do things her way and her way only.

Keon examined the corner of his mouth in the rearview mirror. There was only a light bruise there as a result of one of Dexter's jabs slipping through. The bleeding had stopped, but his desire for revenge was still burning fiercely. He was determined for a rematch once he got his issues with Max resolved. He knew the young buck would be a challenge straight up due to his fighting skills, but there was nothing straight up about his plans for vengeance. Next time he saw him, he would sneak him and make sure he'd regret the day he ever laid a finger on him.

As he repositioned his mirror, he caught a glimpse of Ashley walking out of the hospital, scanning the parking lot for the car. He tapped the horn a couple of times to get her attention. As she slowly began her trek to the vehicle, he said to himself, "Humph, your ass know what's good for you, don't you?"

She eased into the car. He turned to her with a smug look on his face. "I knew you weren't dumber than you look." She bowed her head as he went on to say, "That brother of yours." He began wagging his finger towards her face, "I promise you I'm gonna fuck him up real good when I get the chance—I promise you that. Ain't no nigga gonna get off with handling me that kind a way and not pay for it."

She wanted to smile, but she wasn't crazy enough to do so. She knew it was killing him that he couldn't get back at Dexter, and with him feeling that way, it gave her a sense of redemption. Dexter was able to do some things in that hospital room she had been longing to do for a very long time. However, he didn't he didn't do as much as she'd desired.

****

They didn't go home immediately as they drove around town for hours until dark. Keon cruised around and waited outside Porkchop's mother's house for a while, hoping to catch his homeboy to question him about why he wasn't answering his calls or texts. To his displeasure, there wasn't any activity there, and the residence appeared to be completely abandoned. He then drove around all the places he'd known Angelo to frequent, including all of his baby mother's cribs, and came up with absolutely nothing.

It was like his former crew had dissolved into thin air, leaving him as the sole person to handle their debt with Max.

The ride home was a quiet one as neither said a word to the other. Ashley had absolutely nothing to say to him. Sitting in his presence after what was by far the most brutal attack he had ever made against her, she couldn't help but feel foolish. It sickened her that she left her mom behind at the hospital after she pleaded for her to come back home with her. Her family wasn't stupid. She knew they could tell what really happened, and it embarrassed her. She was so ashamed of herself for running back behind him, but she knew if she didn't, it would only be a matter of time before Keon would show up at her mother's doorstep, at first begging for her to come back to him. If she resisted, he would find some way to threaten her or her family. It was getting to the point that she couldn't underestimate his evil, and she couldn't put the burden of her tumultuous relationship on her family.

He circled around their apartment complex several times before backing the car into a space across from their building. She could tell the paranoia of possibly being watched was getting to him. He was right to worry just from the couple of times she saw Max's men on her own. His eyes bounced from one end of the community to the next in search for anything suspicious in the parking lot. Ashley carried on with her own inspections, also. If someone was waiting or following them, it wasn't the men she'd seen previously.

"Look," he said as he turned off the car. "If I don't get Max his money back to him by tomorrow, we're probably gonna have to leave town for a little while. I'm letting you know ahead of time."

His revelation unnerved her. It just made her more hopeful that he would straighten out whatever he had going on with the gangster known as Max because the last thing she wanted was to be in some foreign place with him.

As they headed upstairs to their apartment, halfway up the steps, Keon stopped in his tracks. "You see that shit," he asked pointing towards their apartment door.

"What?" she asked as she tried to look around him.

"There's a box in front of our door." He nervously looked around the dimly lit corridor to see if anyone was watching them or hiding out in the shadows.

As he continued up the stairs, Ashley followed closely behind. There was a small cardboard box that was sealed with electrical tape sitting in front of their door. They cautiously crept towards the door and stood over the box.

Keon scratched his head as he took a couple of minutes to contemplate what the contents of the box could be. He looked around again, suspicious they were being watched. "Pick it up," he said.

"What?" Ashley answered. She was just as nervous as him. She had no idea why he wanted her to pick up the box.

"It may be my money. Angelo's scary ass may have left it here." Keon now smirking, "His bitch ass is too scared to face me and hand me my shit like a real man, knowing he'd get a fine tuned taste of these hands."

"Or it could be something else… like a bomb."

"Shut the hell up," Keon's smirk quickly disappeared and transformed into an angry scowl. "That nigga ain't gonna leave no damn bomb at the front door. You see how stupid you sound?"

"How do you know it's from him?"

Keon sucked his teeth as he wondered why he was even consulting with her about anything, let alone discussing with her about what was in the box. He considered her clueless about how things were done in the world he was conducting business in. He slowly stretched his leg out and gently kicked the box. Ashley was ready to run on contact, but she was promptly relieved when nothing happened after Keon's contact with the package.

"Pick it up," Keon said. "If it was a bomb, the shit would've blown my fuckin' foot off."

Ashley didn't budge. She just gazed at the box, totally ignoring his request as he scowled her way. Her nerves were wrecked as she knew he wasn't going to rest until she grabbed the package.

"Did you hear me? Pick the motherfucker up."

Stunned, she couldn't believe he was trying to make her pick up a box that only God and whomever left it there knew what was in it. He wasn't man enough to grab the package himself. Instead, he was asking her to put her life at risk by picking it up, knowing good and well whatever it was, it wasn't left for her.

"You want some more of what I gave you yesterday or something?" He cracked his knuckles. "I ain't got no problems hooking you up with some more of it."

She shook her head and placed her focus back on the box. It was going to be hell to pay if she didn't pick it up as he asked. She took a deep breath as she carefully placed her hands on the side of the small package. Trembling, she held it as far away from herself as she possibly could while lifting it.

Keon nervously backed away. "Don't put that motherfucker that close to me."

Before attempting to open the door, he looked around to see if anyone was watching them. He then unlocked the door, pushed it open and told her to go in. Ashley slowly walked in with the box. In her mind it was a bomb, and if she made the wrong move it would blow her up into smithereens. Keon closed the door behind them as Ashley walked to kitchen table and gently sat the box on top of it. She'd already begun perspiring under her arms and forehead in the matter of seconds.

Keon rushed to the kitchen drawer and grabbed a box cutter. They stood at the table with their eyes glued on the package. He was flicking the blade in and out as he considered making her do the honors of slicing it open.

"What do you think it is?" she asked.

"Hell if I know," he answered. "It needs to be my fucking money. That's actually what I think it is. It's probably not all of it, though. Angelo ass must've dropped it off. It ain't gonna save him from this ass whoopin' I got planned for him, though. He can duck and dodge all he wants. It don't matter because he's getting his ass beat—that's a fuckin' fact!"

They continued to ponder over the box quietly for a good five minutes before Keon stepped forward and placed the razor at the top seam of the box. He gave Ashley a quick stare as she took two steps backwards. He then swiped the razor across the center of the box along the middle of the tape and then sliced it along the sides. He gave Ashley one more glance before opening the flaps of the box. There was something inside the black garbage bags that were stuffed inside of it, appearing somewhat the size of a butterball turkey. He ripped the bag from around the object and immediately fell backwards to the floor once his eyes laid witness to Porkchop's bloody, severed head with his eyes carved out. Ashley immediately fell to the floor and threw up.

"Porkchop… Porkchop," Keon cried. He jumped back to his feet, his entire body trembling as he hovered over the box in utter disbelief. "Porkchop, they did this to you, nigga! Oh God, they fucked you up, man. These niggas fucked you up!" He looked towards Ashley with a stray tear sliding down his face and yelled, "They fucked my nigga up… Oh God!"

As she wiped her mouth and stared up at him from the floor, she was unfamiliar with the expression of fear on him. The message Max sent him knocked him down to size, and it put him on notice that he wasn't playing. She then looked towards the box, mystified that someone could butcher another human being the way they did Porkchop. She could only imagine the terrible things they had planned for Keon, and or anyone they thought was close to him. She wanted no parts of it, but she was stuck smack dab in the middle of it.

Several hours had passed, and Keon sat at the table, lost in a trance with the box that he'd now closed the flaps on so he could no longer see the mangled face of his best soldier. After cleaning up the mess she made on the floor, Ashley sat idle on the edge of the couch waiting for him to do or say something besides repeating himself about how he couldn't believe what they did do his friend.

Suddenly, he popped up from his chair with a deranged expression and stomped into the bedroom. She could hear him ransacking the room for a few minutes until things got completely quiet again. When he returned to the living room, he was carrying a big, black gun in his hand. His nose flared from his intensely exhaling. She didn't even know he kept a firearm in the home.

He held the gun up, wagged it around and said, "These motherfuckers think I'm a joke. I ain't going out like no sucka." he looked towards her and added, "You understand that?"

She gave him a soft nod, thinking that he'd finally lost it. He had gone from fearful to delirious. The sight of him with a gun and the crazy expression he wore on his face while toting it scared the daylights out of her.

"This nigga Angelo need to turn up. He need to turn up now." He stuffed the weapon in the small of his back and demanded, "Let's roll. We got shit to do."

Her mouth dropped. Why he thought it would be a good idea to bring her into this situation with people getting their heads chopped off was beyond her rationale. He walked to the table, grabbed the box with Porkchop's head stuffed in it and marched to the door. She hadn't moved an inch.

He looked at her like she was crazy. "What the hell? You gonna sit there all night, or are you gonna move your ass? I told you we got shit to do."

She begrudgingly followed him out of the apartment and down to the car. Prior to leaving the apartment complex, he stopped at the garbage compactor at the front entrance. Before he stuffed Porkchop's boxed up remains in the machine, he looked down at it and promised, "You won't die in vain, my nigga. You won't die in vain."

****

Keon spent most of the day bouncing across town scoping out the residences of Angelo's assortment of baby mothers, and there were no signs of Angelo at any spot. As he advised Porkchop days ago, he figured Angelo would rest his head with the woman he had the most children with and that was Tasha. Angelo had been locked up by her several times in the past for not paying his child support, and it was common knowledge that he wanted to stay in good terms with her to prevent getting locked up again. Besides, he'd always referred to Tasha as his main chick, and the amount of kids he had with her supported that claim.

He cruised around the parking lot of Tasha's apartment complex several times throughout the day but had yet to actually knock on her door to ask her if she knew where Angelo was. After receiving Max's deadly message, he knew it was time to turn things up a notch.

He backed his car into a parking space on the side of the building's entrance that had very little lighting due to the street light being knocked out. The complex consisted of mostly section eight housing, but it was a development where mostly older people resided so it was literally a ghost town at night. When he took a moment to really think about it, the spot was the perfect place for someone in Angelo's situation to be hiding.

"When I'm up in that motherfucker, I need you to be down here with your fucking eyes peeled," he said to Ashley as he turned off the engine. "I don't need you to be falling asleep or your mind wandering, thinking about whatever fucked up fantasy your mind be channeling when you're by your goddamn self. I need you to be watching for shit. If you see that nigga Angelo anywhere in damn sight while I'm up there, I don't give a hot damn if you wake up this whole fuckin' complex, you blow the shit out of the horn so I can get his ass."

He waited for a response, but she didn't give him one. She was too worried about the possibility of getting tied up in some type of homicidal mess now that he was toting a gun around and looking for blood. She didn't want to be an accessory to anyone's murder. Keon was dangling on the deep end, and he was spiraling out of control.

"You fuckin' heard what I said, didn't ya?"

She gave him a nod.

"Then acknowledge what the fuck I'm saying—shit! I don't need your ass to be acting retarded on me now. This shit is real, goddamn it."

He hopped out of the car and headed towards the building's entrance. He didn't leave her sight until he disappeared into the building's stairwell. He climbed up the metal steps with much haste and rage. His search for Angelo, and Max's owed money was bearing down on him immensely. He knew if he came up empty here he would have no choice but to skip town before Max tracked him down.

He crept up to Angelo's baby mother's door and quietly stood in front of it. Putting his ear against the door, he could faintly hear some music. Finally, he knocked.

"Who is it?" a female voice yelled.

"Is Angelo home?"

"Who?"

"Angelo. Is Angelo home?"

After a few moments the music ceased, and he could hear footsteps moving towards the door. The woman on the other side of the door said, "Angelo?

Angelo don't live here? You got the wrong building."

"Tasha, this here is Keon. I don't have time for the bullshit. I need to talk to Angelo."

There was more silence and after a few seconds she said, "Keon?"

"Yeah, Keon, he answered. "You know who this is."

She cracked the door open and peaked through the opening. His head was just above the chain lock that she kept attached to the door. "Keon, you know Angelo don't live here. Besides, I ain't hear shit from him in weeks."

Keon attempted to look over her head to get a glimpse of the inside of the apartment as she rambled on with what he suspected to be all lies. "Damn, Tasha, I thought we went way back. You scared to open the door for a nigga?"

"Keon, you know it's late—nothing personal."

"Nothing personal for you and me, Tasha, but your man, that's another thing. I really need to holla at his ass, Tasha. He got us all tied up in some real serious shit."

"What kind of shit."

"Some serious shit! That's all you need to know," he chuckled then added, "So me and him need to vibe together and figure out how we're gonna work this shit out."

"Well, if I see him, I'll let him know that you're looking for him," she obliged as she attempted to close the door.

Keon slipped his arm through the door. "Nah, Tasha, I need to see that nigga right now."

"Keon, what the fu…" she complained as Keon shoved the door open, snapping the chain latch.

"You just broke my shit. You're paying for that, damn it."

Keon walked into the apartment and whipped out his gun. Her eyes bolted wide open as she took a few steps backwards when she saw the firearm. "Keon, what the hell are you barging up in here with a gun for? Nigga, is you crazy?"

"The kids sleep?" he asked, completely ignoring her question as his eyes scanned every inch of the walls around the living room.

"They at my mommas," she shouted angrily. "Keon, what the hell are you trying to prove, man?"

"That sounds about right," he mumbled to himself as he focused on the hall where the bedrooms were located. "Where the nigga at, Tasha? You know we go back further than you and him. I expect more out of you than for you to be hiding and protecting this lame ass nigga."

"I told you I ain't see him in weeks."

"Don't lie to me, bitch." He pointed the gun at her. "I know you know where the fuck he is."

"Keon, you better get that gun out of my fuckin' face. I know that much, nigga." Tasha was about five feet tall, wearing a pink robe and pink rollers to match.

He took a hard sniff of air and asked, "When you started smoking?"

"I always smoked. How else is a bitch gonna stay relaxed with a sorry nigga and a shitload of kids?"

"Yeah, right," he signaled her with his gun to go to the bedroom area. "Lead the fuckin' way."

"Keon, you can't be doing this," she said as she began leading him down the hallway to the bedrooms.

"I can do whatever the fuck I want as long as that nigga got my fucking money. Now walk slowly to the back. I'm gonna need for you to open them doors nice and slow so I can see for myself if that nigga's here or not. I can't believe shit that you say right about now.

Ashley feared the worst of what Keon could be doing in the building totting around that gun with fear in his heart and a whole bunch of hatred to go with it. She wanted to be brave enough to just jump in the driver side seat and take off without him, but the thought of him catching up to her was the one thing that always plagued her mind, not the fact there could be a possibility that he wouldn't be able to catch up to her. She knew she should've listened to her mother and returned home to her.

From the woods, she noticed a slender man wearing a dark jogging outfit and a hoodie covering his head run up to the same entrance that Keon entered. She couldn't make out if the man was Angelo or not, but he was certainly tall and lanky like him. She considered blowing the horn to alert Keon as he requested, but she wasn't certain if the man was him or not.

Tasha pushed opened the door to the master bedroom, threw her hands in the air and said, "See, I told you he wasn't here. His ass ain't been around in weeks, nigga."

Keon stepped into the room and carefully looked around. He walked to the closet and swung open the door. There was nothing but clothes and mounds of junk stuffed inside from the floor to the ceiling. He took a deep breath and stuffed his gun in the small of his back before punching the wall in fury. Tasha's place was his last hope at finding Angelo and him not being there took everything out of him.

"You got a lot of nerve, Keon, coming into my fucking house with a gun and pointing it all in my face and shit. As much child support that nigga owe me, you think I would be protecting his ass?" she asked as she walked down the hallway towards the living room.

"Damn, Tasha, that's my bad," he said with his head hanging as he followed her down the hall.

"You damn right, it's your bad. A bitch in here trying to get her beauty sleep and you're barging in here worrying me about some sorry ass Angelo!"

The front door swung open. "Tasha, I'm back. Damn store fresh out of rolling papers," Angelo said as he swiped his hoddie from his head and walked into the home with his back turned to Keon and Tasha.

Their mouths were wide opened by the sight of him. Keon couldn't believe his eyes.

"Lying bitch," Keon said.

Angelo turned around to see a red hot Keon standing across the room. It was as if he seen a ghost as he stumbled backwards towards the front door. "Keon... the fuck, man?"

"What's up, nigga?" Keon's high yellow face was redder than a bottle of hot sauce. "Glad you remembered my fuckin' name. Too bad you couldn't remember my fucking phone number."

"Man, I... I...," Angelo couldn't stop stumbling over his words as he slowly began to inch towards the door. Before Keon could make his move on him, Angelo snatched the bookshelf from the wall beside the front door and shoved it to the floor in front of him. He then grabbed the door handle and charged out of the apartment. Upset that she lied to him about everything, Keon shoved Tasha to the floor but he ended up falling over the bookshelf trying to get at Angelo. He quickly made his way to his feet and through the apartment door, hot on Angelo's trail.

Angelo skipped down the stairs to the ground floor as Keon hopped down the steps right behind him. As Ashley waited patiently in the car, she noticed the men running from the apartment building and into the woods. It was then that she realized the man in the dark clothing was indeed Angelo. The first thing she thought about was what Keon would do to her for not warning him when she first saw him entering the building if he didn't catch up to him.

When Keon got close enough to Angelo, he pulled out his gun and threw the pistol directly at the back of his head. Angelo gasped and fell face forward onto the ground. Keon quickly stomped on him in the small of his back causing Angelo to bellow in pain.

"Motherfucker!" Keon yelled, seriously out of breath as he scooped up his pistol. Angelo began pleading with Keon, begging him not to hurt him as he began crawling on all fours away from him. Keon dove down on his back with his knee and smashed him in the back of his head with the butt of the pistol. He hopped up and said, "You turn your fucking ass over! If your ass try to run I'm putting two in you without a second thought, you bitch ass nigga."

"Keon, brotha… I can explain."

"I don't wanna hear that brother shit. I told you to turn your bitch ass over!"

Angelo rolled over frantically and unable to breathe steadily. "Keon, wait, man. A nigga fucked up," he pleaded. "I know you're pissed off at me, man. I'm pissed off at me, cuz."

"Me being pissed off at you is a fuckin' understatement right now, nigga." Keon dropped onto Angelo's chest, cradling him. He stuffed his gun in the small of his back and began pounding Angelo in his face with his bare knuckles. Angelo hollered in pain as his face began to get scarred up and bloodied. "Where's my fuckin' money, nigga? Where is it?"

"Keon… stop, man… stop," he pleaded between punches. "It's not… it's not… what you think… I didn't try to screw you over, man."

Keon pulled back from his onslaught on his weakened prey and looked down at his battered face. The moonlight gave him just enough light to see his handy work, yet he wasn't actually satisfied with the beating so far. "Really, nigga? You ain't try to screw me over? Then what the fuck you call it? You got another name for it?"

"My cousin….Bam…," he said while coughing up blood. "He said he could make some major moves with the cash—major moves! Four times what we had already made off the work we got from Max. He had this partner with really good connections."

"Bam, huh?" he shook his head. He was familiar with Bam and knew him as a bullshitter—always a lot of talk and promises but never any legitimate actions. "So what the fuck happened, nigga?"

There was a pause. Angelo sighed as tears began to flow down his beaten face. "Man…"

"You got fucked, nigga. Your punk ass cousin scammed you out of the goddamn money. My money! You ain't gotta say shit!" Keon backhanded him. "Your stupid ass got us all fucked!"

"Keon, man, wait..man." he cried. "I've been all around town looking for them niggas—trying to get the money back. I was just thinking in the best interests of us, man—the crew. You gotta believe me, man. Brotha!"

"Best interests, huh?" Keon smashed him in his face with a three punch combo and then spit in his face. Angelo didn't make any efforts to fight back. He just helplessly took his pounding.

"Chill man, please," he pleaded while crying like a baby. "I...I know... I fucked... I fucked up."

Keon backed off with his onslaught. "You were thinking in the best interests of Porkchop? You got my nigga head chopped off. So was that in his best interests, nigga? The best interests of your brothers, bitch?"

"Porkchop? Wait, what? What they do? They killed Porkchop?"

"Yeah, nigga they cut my nigga head off and sent the shit to me in a box like it was some priority mail or some shit." Keon hopped up off of him and jumped to his feet. "He dead over your dumb shit, nigga—your dumb shit."

Once Keon climbed to his feet, Angelo sat up on his behind. His face was covered in bruises and blood, but he was relieved that Keon had stopped the attack. He said, "We gotta get the fuck outta here, man. Max ain't gonna let this shit ride if we can't get him his money. We're good as dead if we stick around."

"That I do agree with you on, partna. But there ain't no we in the shit, nigga," Keon said as he removed his gun from the small of his back. Angelo eyes shot open.

Ashley scoured the wooded area where Keon chased the man she believed to be Angelo. She jumped when she heard what sounded like several loud gun shots. Her entire body shook fearfully as she wondered what had happed in those dark woods. Did Keon shoot Angelo or did Angelo shoot Keon? She didn't know what to think. She quickly realized that Keon was no one's victim when she spotted him calmly walking away from the woods and towards the car moments after the gunfire.

Keon jumped into the car. He was heavily breathing, and his hands trembled as he placed them on the steering wheel. After a few moments of silence he said. "I thought I told you to blow the fucking horn when you saw that motherfucker."

"I didn't know it was him," she said softly. She feared he had just killed Angelo in those woods, and she didn't want to be his second kill for the night.

He turned his head towards her, still breathing ferociously. "What the fuck do you know?" She didn't answer him as he just sat and stared at her for a couple of minutes anticipating a reply. Then, he started the car and began making his way out of the apartment complex. After driving a few miles he pulled over to the side of the road. He slipped out his phone and dialed. When he heard the man on the other end of the phone answer, he said to him, "I'm gonna need that thing we talked about."

The low, raspy voice answered back, "Say no more. You know where to be."

Keon ended the call, took a deep breath and looked over to Ashley. "We're gonna have to relocate for a little while."

A stroke of fear drilled down her spine when he mentioned relocating. She didn't want to be with him where they currently resided, let alone being on the run with him to God knows where. She wanted to just tell him no—just no, better yet hell no, but she was just too scared. Her mind couldn't stay in one place because she didn't have a clue as to what was about to happened next. Keon had most likely killed someone, and now he was talking about leaving town, and she wasn't even sure if she was next on his kill list or not.

Keon drove them to a Wal-Mart that was about twenty miles away from their home. He didn't say a word the entire drive. When he initially arrived at the supermarket, he drove around the entire parking lot at least six times before he finally decided on a spot that wasn't too far from the primary entrance. It was late but this particular Wal-Mart was near a couple of college campuses so it was still packed with people.

Keon shut off the car and ordered, "You follow close and don't wander off any fucking where, you understand?"

She gave him a nod, and they exited the vehicle. Keon was so nervous, he couldn't mask his trembling hands and the twitching of his head. When they entered the store, he frequently looked right to left, suspicious of everyone they approached and walked by.

Ashley followed him to the back of the store as Keon carefully and slowly looked down each aisle, obviously looking for something or someone. Once he moved to the sporting goods aisle, they noticed a man in the middle of the aisle observing the bicycles that were hanging from the racks. Keon stopped his stride and stood still for a couple of seconds. The man wore a dark brown Ivy cap and a black leather jacket. He motioned Ashley to remain where she stood as he cautiously approached the middle aged gentleman.

Keon stood side by side with the guy and looked up at the bikes along with him before speaking. "A desperate man can get but so far on only two set of wheels."

The man turned to him and said, "Let's go—quickly!" The man took off towards the back of the store. Keon waved to Ashley to follow them as they headed off into the back. They walked to a fire exit that didn't sound off when the man opened the door. There was a box truck that had its engine running and was parked right next to the door. The man slid the back door upwards and motioned Keon and Ashley to hop into the back of the truck. The man closed them in and looked around to make sure no one was watching them. He then hopped into the passenger side of the truck and the truck took off.

The ride was a bumpy one for the couple as they tried to stay in one place with the crates they sat on. The only light they had was a dim red bulb that hung from the front wall of the truck. Ashley had no idea where they were headed. She was exhausted from the lack of sleep, and she was frightened by not knowing where they were headed. She looked toward Keon who wore an angry scowl on his face as he looked straight ahead at the truck's back door.

"Don't worry. When we get to where we're going you're gonna love it. New place, new surroundings—a brand new start. We could probably even get started on making a little family."

The thought of starting a family with Keon at this stage of their relationship made her want to gag. She looked up at him for a moment wondering if he made the comments as a joke, but his face was straight and serious. She looked towards the floor and thought that there was no way she'd have his baby after all that he'd put her through, even if she had to perform an abortion on herself somehow.

"We wouldn't have to be doing this if you had gotten that fucking money from your momma," he added.

There it was—the real Keon. She knew he'd find some way to blame all of his misfortunes on her. She knew it would come out at some point.

The speed of the truck slowed down. They heard what appeared to be a mechanical door, similar to a home garage door opening but louder. They felt as though they were driving into some type of building as they could hear men just outside of the truck giving the driver instructions as to where to park.

The truck stopped and after a couple seconds of being parked idle, the engine shut down. The doors on both sides of the truck opened and closed from the front of the vehicle. After a few moments of silence, there was banging on the back door of the truck that sounded like it was coming from a metal pipe. They both rose from their respective spots on their crates and crept towards the front of the vehicle. The door slid upwards, and a tall, stocky build man with a short afro and an open sports jacket stood behind two heavy set balled men dressed in two piece suits.

The man removed the short, stub cigar from his mouth and spoke, "You must like it in that motherfucker—you ain't trying to get out."

"Big Percy!" Keon yelled out with a huge smile on his face.

He chuckled and pointed at Keon. "You know better than to call me that shit, ya jackass. You family, but I'll still kick your scrawny little ass. Maybe even do you worst than what Max is aiming to do to you."

"Damn, BP," Keon laughed. "You'll do me like that?" He waved to Ashley to follow him. "Just because your little cuz called you by your goddamn government?"

Keon hopped off the tailgate of the truck, leaving Ashley to struggle to get down on her own.

"I'll do that and a whole lot more, motherfucker," he laughed and embraced Keon with a huge hug. "You dumbass! You got your ass in some brand new dumb shit, I see."

They were in an old body shop. An assortment of cars were scattered throughout the garage—some with their hoods and doors opened, others freshly painted and tricked out, and a few completely hidden under car covers. BP wrapped his arm around the back of his cousin's neck and guided him to his office at the rear of the garage. BP's goons stayed behind as Ashley followed behind the men.

Just before opening the door to his office, BP looked back at Ashley with a bit of a frown. "'Sup, Ashley."

"Hi, how are you BP?"

"Just fine, sweetheart—never better actually. Look here, I gotta talk business with your man for a few. He'll be back in a minute. Have a seat," he said, pointing to the brown sofa just outside his office door.

She took one glance at the old, rugged chair and opted to remain standing with her arms folded. Keon followed BP into the office and shut the door behind himself.

The office was small with an old, shabby desk and a flashy sixty inch high definition plastered on the wall that seemed somewhat out of place with all the other old furniture. There was a huge, tinted window that provided the office a view to the garage area allowing BP to see everything going on in workplace but leaving the work area blinded to him.

While staring at Ashley through the window, BP suggested, "You know it's a lot easier to make this thing work travelling solo."

Keon looked back at Ashley and chuckled, "Yeah, but what the fuck would she do without me?"

"She'd probably live, motherfucker," he laughed.

"Well, ain't nobody dying tonight—especially not my black ass."

"You sure about that nigga?"

"Fuck yeah!"

BP shook his head. "Boy, I told you about doing business with them fuck-boys. You could've been doing business with me, doing organized, thorough business—the type of shit people ain't thinking about and not in the news every goddamn day. But you wanna be a dope boy—a fuckin' dope

143

boy—like it's nineteen ninety-five or some shit." BP took a seat in his executive chair behind the desk. "Fuck you wanna be, Nino Brown?"

"Look, man, I ain't got time for all these lectures and shit. I ain't down with that fucking night club shit, and my mind ain't savvy enough for that credit card shit you got going on."

BP hopped up and leaned over his desk. "But you coming over, *needing my shit*, though." BP sat back down. "You know, Key, a nigga out there wasting his time dope selling on the block, ain't got but a limited amount of time before his dopey ass ends up in some white man's prison doing hard time on his cell block," he chuckled and asked, "Did you even find the nigga that ran off with the money?"

He nodded, instantly furious at the thought of Angelo and the whole ordeal. "Yeah, I found his ass."

"And?"

"I had to put two in him. He got ganked for the dough."

"You're a stupid, nigga, you know that?"

"Yeah, I know."

BP opened the drawer under his desk, pulled out a small, dark satchel and slid it across the desk. Keon grabbed the bag, but he hesitated to do anything else.

"Open the motherfucker," said BP.

Keon unzipped the satchel and pulled out a stack of identification cards and credit cards. A smile arose on his face.

"You know you can't come back here. Not while Max is alive and running these streets. The motherfucker can't stand losing, and he took a loss with your ass. And trust me, it ain't about the money because the bastard got a lot of that. It's the principle. He ain't never gonna let that shit go. Not until your ass is dead."

"Yeah, I know," Keon grinned. "You can always send your dudes to tighten him up for me."

"I'm too old for wars, cousin. I got a family and a good thing going. Besides, if your stupid ass had to have taken me up on my offers and rolled with me, you wouldn't even be in this shit in the first place."

Keon bowed his head and sighed. "Shit, you're right—can't argue that."

"You're family, and this here is the best I can do." BP rose from his chair and walked around his desk to face his younger cousin. He gave him a pat on his shoulder and said, "Wherever you end up, please stop doing dumb shit."

Keon grinned then raised the satchel in front of him and said, "It's appreciated, cuz. It really is. I fucked up, I know that."

"Yes you did," BP nodded and added, "Now get the fuck out of my place before that son of bitch track you here."

"I gotcha'," Keon headed for the door.

Just before Keon could walk out the door to leave, BP stopped him. "The brown Three Hundred parked right at the garage door has the keys in the ignition and a full tank of gas."

"Thanks, cuz," Keon walked out of the office and approached Ashley. "Come on. Let's get the fuck out of here."

****

The interstate was empty under the night sky, and Keon was coasting down it like a bat out of hell. Although they were on the road for a little over an hour, Keon didn't have a specific destination in mind. All he knew is that he was headed west, as far west as he could go to feel comfortable that he was far enough from Max.

Ashley sat quietly on the passenger side. She didn't want to be with him at the place they called home the past few years, and she definitely didn't want to be with him on the run for what could potentially be forever. On the run for something she had nothing to do with. Ultimately, she felt trapped with no way out.

She was at the point that she was no longer angry at Keon but angrier at herself. She couldn't stand the way she always allowed it, and now, she was allowing him to relocate her against her own inner will. She didn't say a damn thing about it—she simply cowered again. She was so fed up with herself, she just couldn't take anymore. It was at that moment her lips released a formation of words that stunned her own ears.

"Keon, you gotta let me out."

He nearly gasped, turning to face her with his mouth gaping open, believing he was hearing things. "What?"

A tear slid down her face. She realized what she said, and she knew there was no way she could step away from it. This was her moment to put her foot down. It was going to be now or never. She continued, "This isn't my fight. I don't know what's going on with you and these gangsters, but it doesn't have anything to do with me." She looked towards him and added, "I don't want to be on the run, Keon."

"Oh my fuckin' goodness," he said, switching his focus back and forth from the road and her. "You must be done lost your fucking mind."

She bowed her head. Something in hopeful her heart thought that he may have responded differently, that for once he'd consider how she felt about things again. She looked straight ahead and kept speaking, "I'm tired, Keon. I'm tired of living in fear. I'm tired… I'm tired of being…" She paused as more tears continued their path down her face. She then looked at him and confessed, "I don't want to be with you anymore. Please, let me out."

He began to laugh hysterically. "Oh my God. Out of all the times in the world you could've pulled this shit." He looked over to her and said, "I guess I need to give you what you're asking for, huh?"

She didn't know what he meant by his words—if he was really going to let her out or if he had something sinister in mind. There was complete silence in the car for at least ten minutes. After a few miles down the highway, he yielded his speed as they approached a dimly lit rest area. He drove the car into a parking space at the entrance in front of the restrooms. The spot was abandoned and a bit eerie with the tall trees surrounding it. If he was really about to let her out, she preferred he let her out at some place like a gas station. The previous exit was about fifteen miles back at it was well lit with plenty stations.

"Whelp, your black ass wanted to go. Here's your stop."

A gush of relief overcame all her fears as she couldn't believe he was actually agreeing to free her of him. It was almost too good to be true. He unlocked the door, but when she grabbed at the handle, he locked it again.

"Keo…"

Before she could finish saying his name, he drilled his fist right to the center of her nose. Her head smashed into the window. He then leaned over her and wrapped both his hands around her neck. "Bitch, how many times I gotta tell you that you'll never leave my ass and live. Huh? Huh, bitch?"

"Keon… Keon, stop," she pleaded. She was frantic as he continued to apply pressure around her neck. She became dazed, and the pain around her neck and head increased immensely while she thought that this moment was the one she expected to come about one day—the day he would try to end her life.

She grabbed him by his wrist, scratching and trying to push him off her. He was so strong and overrun with hatred. He called her all kind of names and demanded she die as he applied more pressure around her neck, telling her that he should've killed her long ago. Ashley began to phase in and out of consciousness as her vision began to blur. She wasn't ready to die, and she surely didn't want to go out by his evil hands. She couldn't die by his hands.

Her fear swiftly turned into anger, and in a last ditch effort to get him off of her, she kneed him in his crotch. The strike propelled him backward into his seat as he grabbed his manhood while squealing in pain. She began stomping at it even harder, smashing his hand, legs and penis repeatedly. She reached over him, unlocked her door and climbed out of the car.

He grabbed her by her foot. The momentum sent her face first onto the pavement. "Bitch, I'mma kill you." He then crawled out of the car behind her and drove his fist to the back of her head. She gulped in agony, but the pain didn't stop her from attempting to crawl away from him.

She continued to claw her way towards the restroom area as he rolled over on his back with his hand massaging his crouch. She finally was able to make it to her feet, and she began to run. Keon also made it to his feet and whipped out his pistol. As she approached the restroom door, he yelled "Stop bitch!" and let off a shot towards her.

"Keon...what!" She froze in her tracks, just in front of the door. She was too scared to turn around to face him fearful he would let off another shot, but this time in her face.

"You stupid, ungrateful bitch," he yelled before shoving her through the bathroom door. She went tumbling to the dingy floor. The bathroom was filthy, barely lit and smelled like a pigpen. "All that I've done for your ass and you want to leave me, bitch! Are you fucking shitting me?" He kicked her in her behind and yelled, "Turn your stupid ass over."

She slowly turned over only to see him pointing his gun right at her face. She cried, "Keon... you don't have to do this."

"Don't tell me what the fuck I don't have to do!"

"All I asked..."

"Bitch—shut up!" He took several deep breaths and continued, "You've been dead weight for far too fucking long."

Just before he could squeeze his trigger, a shot rang out and he dropped his gun. He looked towards his left shoulder and saw that he was bleeding out. He slowly turned around and was greeted with a big white knuckle that propelled him backwards, sending him crashing to the floor next to Ashley.

"Take her outside," said the stocky man. It was the big bald man with the scruffy red mustache from the apartment complex.

The man with him, whom was just as big and stocky as he was, ordered her up. "Come on." He pulled her up from the ground.

"Hey, man what the fuck," Keon yelled toward the man that shot him.

"You know that fuck this is, Robinson. Pay up time."

"Man… look, tell Max I just need a little more time," Keon cried while fearing the worse was about to happen.

"Ain't no more fucking time," said the man as he dove on top of Keon and began pulverizing his face.

Ashley could only get a glimpse of his beating as the other henchmen guided her towards the exit and out of the bathroom. "Sit here," he demanded as he forced her onto the grass. She could hear Keon begging and pleading the man to stop beating him. As she sat there, she feared for her own life but it brought her much pleasure to hear Keon screaming for his. The enjoyment she received from his pain immediately stopped when she heard the three gunshots in rapid succession echo from the bathroom.

After a few moments of silence, the man walked out of the bathroom with Keon's lifeless body over his shoulder. Ashley could only watch the man in fear as he walked towards the car BP had given them and threw Keon's body in the trunk. The black sedan they arrived in was parked right next to the car. She watched the man remove and throw his blood soiled shirt in the trunk with Keon. He then slammed the trunk shut and grabbed another shirt from his car.

Finally, he walked up to his partner and said, "Alright, that's fucking done. Let's get out of here."

"What about her?" The man asked pointing to Ashley.

"What about her?"

"We ain't gonna handle her like we did the rest?"

The man with the scruffy red mustache chuckled and asked Ashley, "Hey, did you see us come here and beat the shit of your boyfriend right before I blew his fucking brains out? Did ya?"

She looked towards the vehicle she rode to the rest stop in and then back at him, prompting her to shake her head.

"I can't hear you."

"No," she said softly.

"I thought not," he said to his partner.   He held out his palm as if he was signaling her to give him something. "Alright, I'm gonna need that back now."

His request stemmed from the night she first saw them passing her by at the apartment, but only they didn't make it all the way out of the apartment complex. Instead, that night the brake lights of the car lit up as the automobile backed up to her as she remained motionless.

**

The man with the scruffy red mustache rolled his window down and said, "Hi, Ashley."

She was befuddled by the man's knowledge of who she was.

"Would you like to do us a favor?" he asked with a devious grin on his face. "One that would actually benefit your life in a whole new way, possibly even extending it. Step a little closer darling."

She remained frozen, terrified to move one single inch. He waved her closer with a pistol after his initial request fell upon deaf ears. "Sweetheart, if I wanted to kill you, I could've gotten you right before you saw us while you were struggling with that big ass bag of trash. Could've popped you right in the head. You wouldn't have known what hit ya'."

She slowly walked a few steps closer, convinced that the bald man could've indeed ended her if he desired.

"Good girl," he smiled.

"What do you want?"

"We may need your help."

"Why would I help you? I don't even know you?"

"That is true. You don't know us, but your man does," he said. "And like I said a few moments ago, helping us can only help you. You see, I don't know if he let you in on this or not, but your little boyfriend back there is in debt with my boss for a substantial amount of money, so much, we're beginning to get the feeling that he's not going to be able to pay up before his deadline."

"And what does that have to do with me?"

"Everything, sweetheart," he said. "You see, guys like us, we get paid to observe and eventually execute. So while we've been observing Mr. Robinson the last couple of weeks, we started noticing that you don't appear to be a particularly happy woman. Now, if you've been observing things about your man like we've been observing things about him in this very short period of time, we're pretty certain that you're aware that his time ain't that exclusive to you."

She held her head in shame as the man insinuated Keon was cheating on her.

"We figure if he decides to run, maybe you can help us out, and in return, we can take some of that drama out of your life... and we can even assure you that you'd have a life to have the drama removed from." He removed the aim of his gun from her and held up a black device that resembled a thumb drive. "You see this right here? This fancy little do-hickey is what they call a GPS tracker. All we need for you to do is turn this little contraption on if he tries to sneak off with you somewhere without us knowing and then we'll handle the rest." He threw her the gadget.

She observed it carefully after she caught it. After giving the gadget a quick look over, she looked at him and questioned the whole idea, "If I don't?"

He shrugged his shoulders and momentarily bobbled his head with a silly look on his face. "Well, that's your decision, sweetheart. I just can't guarantee you we'd be this sociable with you the next time we meet, that's all." he said. "Besides, why wouldn't you?" he laughed. "We'll be seeing you, Ashley." He drove off.

***

Ashley dug into her pocket and handed him the tracker.

"Thank you, sweetheart," said the man as he stuffed the contraption in his pocket. "A deal's a deal. It's been nice working with you, Ashley." He turned to his partner and said, "Let's get the fuck outta here."

She watched the men walk away as they took off with their car and the car BP gave Keon. She then climbed to her feet, took a deep breath and gazed back at the restroom. Keon was finally gone. She began walking towards the main highway.

She sat on the edge of the walkway, just in front of the door of a twenty-four hour gas station she discovered at the exit a few miles down from the rest stop. She sat silently—hair mangled lips sore and busted along with a throbbing pain along her rips. With her hands clasped together on top of her knees, she ignored every late night patron that found their way into the spot, whether they had genuine concerns about her battered and bruised face or if they merely thought she was a late night trick looking for a John to pick her up.

It wasn't until a late model Mercedes rolled into the parking space next to her that she made any movement. She hopped up and briefly gazed into the lightly tinted windows of the luxury car. She then approached the passenger side door and opened it, easing into the ride.

"Did they get him?" asked the driver.

She turned towards the driver and calmly replied, "They got him, Ma."

"Well, I guess I shouldn't have doubted you when you said you could take care of things back at the house."

Ashley let out a deep breath, totally exhausted by the events of the past few days. Then, she let back her seat and motioned forward. "Let's just go home, Ma."

"You got it sweetheart," Rose smiled, relieved to finally have her daughter back. As Ashley reclined in her chair with her eyes closed, her mother scanned her over, enraged and woeful over the bruises that sprawled across her daughters face and arms. She gave her daughter a gentle rub on her knee before backing out of the parking space, grateful she had her daughter back.

THE END

UGLY (Preview)

He stood in front of the mirror with his head hanging down as he hovered over the bathroom sink with both arms stretched out against the wall. He had been positioned that way for a little bit over a half hour. He was fully dressed in his usual attire–black hoodie, baggie blue jeans and boots. It was another first day and another new school with a brand new group of potential tormentors. Julius had been dreading this day for months–three to be exact–ever since the day him, his mother, and his good for nothing stepfather moved into this new place.

Although his mom provided her best efforts to talk up the new school, there was no hiding the fact that Washington High was known for being one of the worst schools in the entire district, and possibly the whole state. But the rent here was good and his mother was hopeful that this school would be different for him than all the rest.

The neighbors told her many positive changes had come to the troubled institution near the end of the previous school year resulting from the successful basketball program there. They also told her that the school board had brought in a mostly new staff and a hardnosed veteran principal that didn't take any shit and that he was calling all the shots.

It made Julius no difference because he didn't play any sports, and he did his best to stay out of people's way, more specifically school staff. This was his senior year, and as with every school year, he was determined to do what he had to do to make it go by as quickly and as smoothly as possible. Of course, with his looks, he often found that task extremely difficult to accomplish.

He slowly lifted his head and gazed into the mirror. He had hoped when his eyes returned to the reflection in that spotty old bathroom mirror another face would appear. A handsome face. A likeable face. Any face but his.

Big nose, huge lips, jet black skin and a bumpy forehead. He knew he was stuck with three out of four of those features for life, but even a complete surrender on drinking sodas and eating sweets did nothing to smoothen out his rough skin.

He swiped a towel hanging from the shower rack and began dampening it. He gently applied the cloth to his face and then began to violently scrub his face with it. His intention was to wipe his face completely off of his head, but he was unsuccessful again. He tossed the towel across the shower rack and sorrowfully stared at himself in the mirror once more. *Why me?*

✶✶✶✶✶✶✶✶✶✶✶✶✶

Vince sat at the table with his legs crossed and a newspaper hanging over his lap in the center of the small kitchen. The hair on his bronzed colored head and face looked like an army of buck shots was etched onto it as he hadn't done anything with himself in the past two weeks. Most days he didn't even make an effort to slip out of his wife-beater and jogging pants–his normal around the house attire.

"They say Michael Jordan is gonna redeem himself this season. His ass shouldn't have left in the first place," he said as he flipped to the next page in the sports section of the paper. "Talkin' about he wanna go play baseball. I guess he found out quick that shit wasn't for him."

"You know he was going through some things with his father's death and all. He just needed some time to sort things out," Felicia said. She was posted at the sink, scrubbing a frying pan amongst the pile of unwashed dishes that were spread out across the counter. It wasn't unusual for her to be the last one to get to bed and the first one up in the morning, just in time to have Vince his morning ham and cheese omelet ready so he could stretch out and read his morning newspaper.

In addition to making Vince his breakfast every morning, the middle aged, brown skinned woman was responsible for doing the previous night's dishes and all the housekeeping duties also. Despite Vince being home all day, every day, he did absolutely nothing but wait for her to come home and get supper ready.

The petite woman was clearly a fox in her day, with her slanted eyes, full lips and flawless brown skin, but working a full time job and taking care of the house was beginning to take its tiresome toll on her. A few days ago she began noticing small clumps of her hair falling out. She simply blew it off as a result of aging and the stress from the extra burden of having to take care of all the bills while Vince was out of work.

"Hell, I need some time to sort things out," he said while closing the paper and slinging it across the table. "Like what am I gonna do if these people don't call me back for some more hours on this damn job? Tucker nor none of them niggas called me about working any routes since we moved here."

"They'll call. They always do."

"How the hell they gonna call if the phone get cut off? We keep going this direction they gonna get cut off any day now. You asked them people for some more hours yet?"

"I've been asking for weeks now, but everybody is in the same crunch we're in, and they ain't trying to get up off their hours. I may be able to

167

fill in for Rita today, but Lance has to call me and let me know something first."

"Well, something needs to give. Shit!"

Julius walked into the kitchen toting his notebook. His notebook was like an extra arm to him, and he rarely went anywhere without it. He strolled to his mother and gave her a quick peck on her cheek. "Good morning, Ma."

"Hey, baby," she replied as she leaned into his kiss, not removing her hands from the sudsy dish water.

Vince's face transformed into one of disgust the very second Julius walked in. His eyes zeroed in on the boy as he moved from his mother to the refrigerator. Julius grabbed a carton of milk and poured himself the remaining portion from the carton. He could feel Vince's beady eyes cutting through his back as they did every morning. He made certain not to make any eye contact with the old grouch, but it didn't matter because Vince had all eyes on him.

"I saw kids walking to school about twenty minutes ago," Vince griped. "It's not gonna be the same shit you pulled at Hampton down here. That's a good ten minute walk to that school, so I suggest you be there on time, every morning. Ain't nobody got time be talking to no teachers and no counselors this year. Your momma ain't gonna do it, and I'm damn sholl ain't gonna do it."

Julius simply guzzled down his milk as if Vince wasn't even there. He knew the guy wanted a fight, but he decided it was best not to even follow the old man up. An argument with him would only lead to a bigger squabble between him and his mother in her efforts to keep peace between the two. He understood his mother had enough on her plate with working a full time job and cleaning up behind practically two grown men, than to have to go through another unnecessary war of words with Vince again.

"You can act like you don't see me. You can even act like you don't hear me. But you better damn well remember what I say goes around this here place."

Julius sat his glass in the sink as he cut his eye at Vince. The temptation to spit fire back at his common law stepdad was there, but he reneged. "Later, Ma."

As Julius made his way towards the side door to leave, Vince shot across the room and grabbed him by his arm. "Boy!"

"Vince," Felicia called out, wanting the dispute to end as fast as it started. She grabbed a towel from off the counter to dry her hands and approached the two.

"Man, what's wrong with you?" Julius questioned.

"Don't you ask me what's wrong with me," Vince grunted. "It's gonna be a lot wrong with you, you keep on playing with me, acting like you don't hear me. You gonna make me stomp a mudhole in your deformed looking ass."

"Vince, leave him alone. Please!" Felicia begged.

Vince looked over to Felicia with a scowl as he continued to place his firm clutch on the boy's arm. He looked back at Julius and gave him an inviting smirk, practically daring him to do something as he tightened his grip.

"Get off me!" Julius yelled as he snatched his arm away.

"Oh, I ain't on your ass, yet," Vince warned him, his eyes piercing through the young man like a savage lion on the brink of attacking some unexpected prey in the wilderness. Even though Vince hovered over Julius by an entire foot, the old bully was ready for certain victory. He yearned for the day that Julius would swing back at him. That would be the same day he would unleash severe pain on the teen, the day he'd been attempting to trigger for years. Fortunately for Julius, he never bit.

"Go ahead and head off to school, Julius," Felicia said as she gave her son a small pat on his back directing him towards the door.

Julius stood firm, contemplating smashing Vince in his grungy face a few good times with his notebook, but the chance of him swinging and missing frightened him. Vince's smirk transformed into a chuckle. He knew Julius didn't have enough nerve to make a move, and he rejoiced in that knowledge. Julius pulled his hood over his head and reluctantly left the house, slamming the door behind himself. Vince happily looked on as Felicia stood before him infuriated.

"I thought I told you to leave him alone in the morning."

"Ah, I ain't did nothing to the boy," he said as he waved her off and reclaimed his seat at the table. "He needs to be toughened up a bit anyway. Won't have to be crying about what them people at that school got to say about him all the time."

****

Washington High was a much bigger school than any Julius had attended in the past. Despite the school's notoriously bad reputation, the outside of the institution was well kept and the halls were spotless. He could smell the new paint from the freshly painted walls as he moved through the halls.

The halls were filled with students laughing and joking with each other, just like any school. Some kids were wandering down the long halls, staring up at the room numbers plastered over the door of each room to find the right class. Others stood posted up alongside their lockers as if they didn't have a care in the world. Julius briskly walked down the hallway with his hood covering most of his

171

face as his eyes stayed glued to the floor. No eye contact always meant no problems.

"You gotta take that hood off in the building, son," said a man pointing a walkie-talkie straight at Julius as he approached him from the other end of the congested hallway.

Julius stalled with his movement for a moment as he looked up and made brief eye contact with the stout man. He didn't look like a teacher with his cheap pleated slacks and black sports coat, but he was making demands like he was a figure of authority. Julius thought he was just a hall monitor or somebody, so he quickly swiped his hood from over his head and heeded to the man's request. The man made his way past Julius, and he continued on his way down the hall once he recognized Julius obeyed his command. Julius kept his stride in his own direction, and after realizing the man was well on his way down the hall and not paying him anymore attention, he quickly whipped his hood back over his head. Julius felt naked walking around the school grounds without his hood covering up most of his face. He hated the feeling of people staring, pointing and laughing at him as they did so many times in the past.

Julius strolled into the classroom that was assigned to be his home room. He didn't have to wander around for any of his classes because when his mother signed him up to the school earlier in the summer, he surveyed all the spots most of his classes would be. The only class that wasn't in the same vicinity as the majority of his courses was his art class. His art class was on the other side of the building near the cafeteria.

He made it his business to get into the school's art class over gym. Art was his first love, and although he was in good physical shape, he wasn't very athletic. Art gave him an escape from how he felt about himself on the outside, and it was an opportunity for him to release the beauty he sustained on the inside. Not for anyone else, simply for himself.

Only a handful of students were sitting in the room, and they paid him no attention as he sought out his destination to the desk in the back of the room.

Julius immediately opened his notebook and began working on a sketch of a street hoodlum he had started the night before. With each stroke of his pencil, his mind reflected more and more on Vince. How he longed for his mother to drop Vince and kick his worthless ass to the curb. It pissed him off to see the old man reclining on the sofa each day while his mother worked her butt off to pay the bills without any help from him. It irked him even more because he was too scared and too undersized to put Vince in his place.

"Hey, is anybody sitting here, man?" asked a voice from the desk to his right.

Julius looked up and noticed a frail boy wearing a bright orange polo shirt had claimed the chair beside him. This shocked him because in all his

173

years of public education, no one had ever sat beside him freely, they'd always have to be assigned the seat. "Nah, nobody sitting there." Julius went back to his artwork and despising Vince.

"You must be new here. I never seen you before," said the boy.

"Yup," he said, not removing his focus from his artwork.

"Well, my name's Trey," said the boy as he extended his fist.

Julius looked up, puzzled by the boy's kindness. He glanced at the boy's hand, dropped his pencil and gave him pound. "Julius."

"Nice to meet you, Julius. What school you coming from?"

"A couple of different spots."

"Your family military?"

"Nah, poor."

The boy chuckled. "I'm familiar with that. Man, that's some smooth artwork you got going on there."

"Yeah," Julius answered, still puzzled by the boy's kindness. The boy had a low, box haircut and was as thin as a dime. He didn't look like a playboy nor a jock, so Julius figured him to be a nerd or some type of outcast. But even nerds and outcasts normally strayed clear from Julius due to his looks.

"I know you gotta be in Mr. Bass's art class with skills like that."

"Yup," Julius answered as a young lady walked in with a couple of girls at the front of the class. The moment he laid eyes on her it was like everything had started to move in slow motion. The small talk Trey was shoveling became mute as his eyes followed the pecan brown tanned girl to her seat. She walked in with two other girls, both were cute, but neither could hold a match to her beauty.

"That's Simone Wilson." Trey's last statement broke through Julius' deaf ears. "Finest chick in the school."

Julius focused back on Trey, "She a cheerleader?"

"Was," Trey answered. "They say she stopped because she wanted to just focus on her books and get ready for college, but she's fine *and* smart as hell. I think she was just trying to stay out of the view of that asshole, Ricky Smith."

"Who's Ricky Smith?"

He chuckled. "Nobody but the pride and joy of Washington High. He's the star basketball player that thinks his shit don't stink."

"Oh, one of those types."

"Yeah, he's bad news man. He wanted her but she didn't want him, and he can't seem to get over it. Dude thinks he owns the place. I can't stand his ass."

Julius takes another glance at the beautiful girl that's managed to captivate his mind in the matter of seconds. He knew he would never have a chance with her, but he couldn't help but think, *what if?*

First Degree Sins (Preview)

By Mirika Mayo Cornelius

"So his name is Nathaniel Cylinders?" I ask, but I don't expect Candyce to answer. Therefore, I give her my own plan. "That's a great plan, Candyce, but before you get out, I'm taking my half of the money. What's mine is mine. I'm no thief." I know it sounds stupid as hell, but I'm really not a thief. A reactive killer as of recent, but not a thief. "You might just try to get away with him but remember, if you take off in that car without me, Smack will be laying smack on that ground like some smack." Truth is, I'm just calling Candyce's bluff. I've never been offended in Smack. I really do love the dog, so I'm leaning on Candyce believing me based off of my prior killings…well, the ones that she knows about. "When I drop you off at the bench, I'm going around the block where I can see you through the trees. When I see you get in the car, you need to circle the block until you see this car. When you do, let the door swing open and I'll jump in. You better remember that I have your loaded gun on Smack the whole time."

"Don't kill my baby, Lisa. Don't kill my baby," she cries, but her cries end soon as I pull up to the Waffle House. It's packed as usual, however, I don't wait on anyone to see how frantic I look, so I press on the gas to drop Candyce off at the suicide bench.

"Wait, I can't get out."

"Try your best because I can't get out either."

As I watch Candyce pull herself up by the door's handle, she pulls her hair back into a ponytail. Then she looks down at Smack with a crooked smile, and then the smile fades when she looks at me. Good thing I have on my sunglasses. I look away.

"What happened? That's the least you can tell me before you let me out. You fucked my hair and face up, so go on. Tell me."

I don't hesitate to tell her. What else can she do when I have the love of her life cradled in my arms with a pistol waiting to fire? Checking the road both ahead and behind me, I make the conversation quick. That's the least I can do although I'm shaken as fuck. I have to play like I'm hard as hell so my dear friend who has miraculously survived the attack won't try anything to save her own life.

"I caught Robert in bed with one of his girlfriends after they ate the dinner I cooked for him. I'd set the table and all, but when he got home, he beat my ass, hence my black and red eye. When I left, I decided to go back. That's when I caught him in bed, both their clothes off, and he told her that he loved her. I slit her throat, stabbed his ass up and then I left. I forgot some of the other stuff, but I went shopping for Smack some food. Then you called me on the road when I was pulling your car in the garage, saying you were being late. Then, when I got in, I had to make a run for it because the cops and everyone on the street was in front of my house. I left your car there and took my car elsewhere. Now, we're here and you're getting out to come pick me up in a different car." I turn my eyes back to look her in the face and her mouth is wider than an elephant's head. "Bye." I turn to face the road, ready to drive ahead. "I'll see you in twenty minutes." She hands me my sum of money and takes the left over in her bag. Then, she looks outside the window.

"This is suicide bench."

"Get out of the car!" I scream directly inside of her beat up face. I can even see traces of ash from the ashtray on her cheekbone as she stares at me like I'm not supposed to let her out at the bench. "What?" I yell. "It was your man's idea! Get out!"

More Akirim Press Books

Books by Rod Cornelius

Diggin' Gold

The Trusted

Single Again

Ghetto Eyes

The Best Kept Secrets

When It Comes Around

UGLY

Whatever It Takes

Books by Mirika Mayo Cornelius

Secret

Colored Lily: Poppa Took My Innocence

Ain't Quite What I Thought

Ain't Quite What I Thought 2

Sunny Sides of My Shade

Murders At Gabriel's Trail: The Complete Series

First Degree Sins

Paton

Books by Cyan Deane

Dead Man's Mayhem

Execution's Karma